"'Touching' and 'cyberpunk' might not often intersect, but they do with Digital Extremities. It swings from moving to haunting in an instant, searching for our humanity in an increasingly dim future. Bassett both honours the legacy of the genre while keeping one fixed firmly on new horizons with a collection which spans the world."
—**Timothy Hickson** of Hello Future Me, author of *A Catalogue for the End of Humanity* and *On Writing and Worldbuilding Vol. I-III.*

"Digital Extremities is a beautifully written collection that explores the intersection of technology and everyday life. Highlighting the narratives of ordinary people navigating a future where tech has become an inseparable part of physical bodies, these are elegant, poignant stories told with organic heart."
—**Suzan Palumbo**, author of *Countess* and *Skin Thief: Stories.*

"Adam Bassett displays a clear talent for world-building and a keen eye for character."
—**T.R. Napper**, author of *Neon Leviathan*, *36 Streets*, and *Aliens: Bishop.*

"There's a depth to the characters that really made this collection shine. [Some] stories made me wonder about future

possibilities, and others that felt real enough to be happening *now*."

—**A.J. Calvin**, author of The Caein Legacy and The Relics of War series.

"Adam has done a wonderful job of exploring a near future where our experiences have become so dominated by technology that it seems impossible to distinguish between the physical world [from] the digital one. Despite [that], these stories remain anchored in the humanity of their characters."

—**B. K. Bass**, author of *What Once Was Home* and editor for *Digital Extremities*.

"*Digital Extremeties* packs a pensive punch in just a few bite-sized stories, all of which invite the reader to look beyond the shining chrome and indispensable convenience of body modification and confront the potential ramifications [that] technological advancement brings. Far from a collection of heavy-handed cautionary tales, Bassett has created a wonderfully thoughtful and at times unsettling cyberpunk setting where everything from the characters' personal relationships to their memories can be manipulated by technology—for better or for worse."

—**Emory Glass**, author of *Thirty-Three Tales of War* and *Fall, Sacred Apple*.

"*Digital Extremities*...will take you through the gamut of emotions and leave you heartbroken, hopeful, and sometimes reeling with existential dread (in a good way)."
—**Beth Heyn**, author of *Marked by Moonlight*.

"Prepare yourself to be moved one moment and deeply uneasy the next. This is a very real experience we're hurtling towards... [*Digital Extremities* is] genuine and pragmatic. A worthwhile read without a doubt."
—**Tom Bookbeard** of FanFiAddict.

"This was a wicked collection of unique, original, engaging short stories. Each take is deeply immersive, but the anthology as a whole reads as cohesive."
—**A. Atkins**, author of *Them Bones*.

DIGITAL EXTREMITIES

STORIES BY
ADAM BASSETT

eBook ISBN: 979-8-9909819-0-4
Paperback ISBN: 979-8-9909819-1-1

Cover Illustration by Igzell
Cover Design by Adam Bassett
Map Illustrations by Adam Bassett

First Edition 2024

Contents

For Mom & Dad, whose incessant belief in me is just a little bit intimidating.

About Content Warnings

Although I would consider *Digital Extremities* appropriate for most ages, the stories are intended for mature audiences and do contain some content and references that may be off-putting to some.

If you would like to see the content warnings before reading this book, skip to the end, where I've listed each story's content warnings as spoiler-free as possible.

Alone / Together

Burlington, Vermont — 2089

Above the haze of city lights, the sky was black and starless. Carl knew there was more out there than he could see, but knowing such things didn't change the empty void outside his bedroom window.

He stood, careful not to wake his wife, and walked to the kitchen, only to remember the fridge was barren. Carl considered the whiskey, then thought better of it, and poured himself a cup of water. It tasted *off*. He left it half-empty on the counter.

He found his sleeping pills in the spare room on top of a hand-me-down dresser. He and Sayra received it as a gift from a neighbor after Sayra became pregnant. It was heavy—made of real wood—with large, white knobs. It was scuffed and dented, worn by years of use. A can of varnish sat beside it on the floor, unopened. A wide paintbrush, still new, rested atop its cover.

Carl glared at the bottle of sleeping pills. They expired a year ago. The instructions called for one; he took two and swallowed. They went down hard.

He stood there a moment, staring at that dresser.

Inside the drawers there was nothing but air.

Sayra considered getting out of bed, but the very idea made her stomach turn. As if her body hadn't already betrayed her enough. She spent another morning mulling over what had happened, amazed at how quickly she'd run out of options.

She felt she was the only person without any left.

The blind purchased new eyes. Amputees received limbs. All manner of cables could help people interface with any network under the sun for work, pleasure, or anything else. And those were just the utilities. Cozmods had come a long way in recent years, adapting to new markets wanting to shed a bit of their humanity in favor of something more stylish. A woman could implant lights beneath her skin that changed color on a whim, or dye her body green and replace her vocal cords for a better pair. In the last twenty years, the music industry had split down the middle—one half seeking the perfect sound, the other contracting only natural voices.

Sayra had gotten caught up in all of that, even here in the mountains.

She'd arrived when the waves began to lap up against the Sunrise Highway, just blocks from where she grew up in Massapequa. They'd said that was the furthest the oceans would rise, but it was underwater now. Only by an inch, but that was enough to turn the place into a ghost town.

New York City was fine, though. They'd walled it off years ago. No money was left in the budget for the rest of Long Island, apparently.

Tech could fix someone's most severe ailments, make them look or sound however they wanted, and even hold back oceans so people in cities could go about their lives as though nothing had changed—when they wanted to, anyway.

But where were the advancements for mothers? Why was it that people could be reconstructed practically from scratch, and yet there was an empty room just across the hall? An empty room with an empty crib and an empty dresser for somebody who never got to live a day of their life.

It was all too much.

Too cruel.

Carl tried to rouse her at some point. She pretended to be asleep, and he let her be. Sayra knew her husband meant well, and that he was hurting, too, but she couldn't get up, and she couldn't console him. Sayra didn't have it in herself to even try.

She just needed to rest, but doing so weighed her down with guilt. Speaking with her husband *should* be within her reach. She *should* be able to eat without having to starve herself first. Instead, she was making him go through this alone. She loved him for helping her and hated herself for not being able to do more. Do *anything*.

The half dozen missed calls from her friends and family only made it worse. Jen had tried again only hours ago. Sayra was glad that Jen hadn't given up on her, even though she absolutely should have. *Sayra* would have.

She needed it to end.

A part of her knew that was a dangerous thought, one that was best untouched, but it came back to her every time she tried to open her eyes.

There were several therapists in the city, as well as doctors who advocated a short list of vaguely familiar medications. Sayra blinked through a list on her lens, a thin device that sat on her eye and displayed information in augmented reality. Doctors' names and biographies floated over her view of the window, its dark curtains drawn over the afternoon sun.

She always found something to critique. The doctor was too far, too expensive, or her insurance didn't cover her visit. The medication was too severe, had terrible side effects, or only concealed the darkness that threatened to swallow her from morning to night. She didn't need it hidden, she needed it gone.

It wasn't until midafternoon–after she refused lunch again–that Sayra found something that looked promising: Recollections LLC. The dark blue logo flickered against the curtains. The company was new in town, but she recognized the name from Long Island. There wasn't a lot of information on her lens, but she recalled some aunts and uncles talking about how their surgeons removed the memories of the floods and helped them move on with their lives.

It was just enough to get her out of bed. Sayra dressed in some clothes that had been lying on the floor and found her bus pass beside them.

Carl asked where she was going. She wasn't sure she wanted to talk to him about it yet, so she said she was going out for some air, which wasn't entirely untrue. She'd been in the house for a week. It would probably be good to walk around the city a bit.

"Oh," he said. "Great. Do you want some company?"

"I don't think so. I just need some time."

"Okay." He nodded. Whether or not he understood the sentiment, she couldn't tell. "I'm going to go pick up a few things then, I think. We're low on water and out of food. Anything you want?"

"No," Sayra said. She paused in the doorway, staring down the long metal staircase. "Whatever you get will be fine."

Sayra left the building, exiting beside the old brick diner. The apartment she shared with Carl had been built on top of it a few years ago as part of a larger housing project that saw the new city rise on the bones of the old. The whole street looked like that: old wood or brick buildings, some built centuries ago, topped with cookie-cutter apartments. Some stretched four or five stories high, battling the trees for sunlight.

She walked a few blocks to the bus stop. It was a small enclosed space with an ancient wooden bench inside, littered with paper flyers advertising community plays, craft shows, and a missing cat named Suki.

The bus arrived a few minutes later. It seemed too wide for the narrow roads, as if it might catch a mailbox or passing vehicle at any moment, yet the driver was at ease. He leaned back and cast Sayra a glance as she climbed aboard.

"Afternoon," he said as Sayra found a seat.

The old faux leather was cool to the touch and tearing at the seams.

Carl meditated on the mundane act of existing in a grocery store, his cart pulled off to the side in aisle three beside the soy sauce. There were twelve kinds to pick from. Some were dark, others tamari, and some had no label at all other than *soy sauce*. Most of the labels were in English. A few were in Japanese. An ad appeared on his lens offering to translate the text if he upgraded to the premium plan. He dismissed it and tossed a bottle into the cart.

He liked the dragon illustration along the label.

These were the little moments of control he'd been missing. That was the thesis of his grocery-based meditation, he decided. That was why he was using the sleeping pills and why he'd put so much energy into trying to help his wife—not that he needed a reason to help Sayra during such a traumatic time, but it felt good to have an explanation for things. The same way it felt good to be making simple, boring decisions again. It didn't matter what kind of soy sauce he got. Neither of them would notice a difference.

After being cooped up at home—after everything he and Sayra had been through—it felt like things were finally inching their way back to normal, whatever that meant now.

Sayra opened her eyes just as a flashing light faded away. A headache split through her skull in its wake.

She sat in the maw of a machine that enveloped her head, its arms unfolding and revealing her to the world now that its work was done. She knew what the device was and what it did, but the memory of how she got there was gone.

"How're you feeling, Mrs. Camirin?" the doctor asked. He was dressed in a simple lab coat. Chrome folded all around his eyes, head, and arms. The tech was reminiscent of the mods she and Carl—and most other people—had installed. However, where they had simple slots to import and export data on the side of their heads, the doctor looked like he had crawled out of a science fiction film. His eyes were covered by a complex visor that seemed too large for his body, the name *Recollections LLC* debossed between the lights where his eyes should have been. Cables ran from his temples and the base of his skull into the machine that Sayra sat in, bright blue and green lights illuminating his hair and shoulders.

Sayra grunted in response and turned away from the lights.

"Of course," the doctor said. "Here, take these pills. You'd think after all these years I'd stop asking stupid questions! No, take two. They'll ease the pain. The next twenty-four hours are crucial, Mrs. Camirin. Do not stress yourself. Relax. Rest, and come morning, you'll be feeling much better. Oh, and when you leave, best to go the back way. Protesters out front won't be kind to that headache. Or wait them out in the lobby. There's usually room somewhere."

"Thank you," Sayra said, a bit uncertain what she was thanking the doctor for, but then—that just meant the operation had been successful. The spidery machine had removed a memory.

When she left the operating room, Sayra expected Carl to be waiting for her, but she didn't recognize anyone in the waiting room. A receptionist got Sayra's attention and slid a small black case across the counter. It contained a flash drive, the kind that could easily slot into the reader in her head.

"Your discarded memories are the property of Recollections LLC, but if you need a peek at what you removed just pop that in," he said. "You don't have to look at it if you don't want to—not everyone likes to know why they came to us—but it's there if you want to."

"Thanks," Sayra said, sliding the thin black case into her coat pocket.

"Just don't come back asking to remove the memory of reading it," the receptionist continued, his attention diverted by something on his lens. A flash of red flitted over his eyes. "Removing a memory doesn't work so well the second time. The company avoids it as much as it can. So, if you decide to look, you'll have to live with whatever you see there."

Sayra took a deep breath. She felt as though she'd been handed a live grenade. The pin was still in, but it seemed too feeble a way to prevent an explosion.

"Thanks," she said again.

Sayra walked out through the back door. The protesters were out in full force, chanting, "Our memories are not for sale!" and "Corponauts, corpo-not!" Between that and the traffic, she could feel the migraine getting worse.

As she made her way toward the bus stop, a pit grew in Sayra's stomach. What had been so bad that she needed to remove the memory of it? Was it something she'd done to herself? Had somebody hurt her, or had it been an accident? Sayra trusted she must have had her reasons.

Carl always made fun of her for needing to think every little decision through, yet she was leaving Recollections clutching her memories in her pocket. She didn't know if she could even talk to her husband about it. He hadn't come to pick her up, which suggested he didn't know what she'd done. That made two of them, she supposed.

Or, Sayra wondered, was the memory of something that happened to *him*? She thought back to the last few weeks and could remember glimpses of her life with Carl: eating dinner together and him waking her up to go to the bathroom at night. Nothing stuck out as unusual. Nothing was out of the ordinary.

Carl was probably fine, but she still wondered about his absence. That was unlike him. When they started trying to conceive, he went with her to every consultation, even when she insisted he didn't have to. When his niece was in the hospital, he spent his lunch breaks visiting and playing cards with her.

As she arrived at the bus stop, Sayra decided to keep whatever had happened a secret, at least until she knew more. If she ever learned more. She ran a finger along the edge of the flash drive's case, tempted to slot it in and see what she'd erased, but she couldn't bring herself to do it. Certainly not in public.

Instead, she stood in silence, listening to the autumn wind.

Carl was glad to see Sayra on her feet and getting out of the apartment again. She'd spent too much time cooped up since the miscarriage. Both of them had. She looked tired as she left the restroom, but that made sense, given all that she'd been through lately.

"What do I smell?" Sayra asked.

"Dinner," he said, watching her closely as she walked into the kitchen.

"Thank God. I'm starving."

It wasn't anything special, but the stir fry tasted good. He'd mixed some thinly-sliced chicken with carrots, rice, and bell peppers. Over it, he spread soy sauce and synthetic honey with a few spices blended in. An old recipe, and an easy one to make, but it always tasted good.

"Where did you go on your walk today?" he asked as they sat down together.

She shrugged the question off. "Nowhere. Around the block. Lost track of time, or I would have been home sooner."

Carl knew she was lying. If that was all that had happened, she wouldn't have been so dismissive. Under normal circumstances, she would have spent the next half hour talking about her day, detailing all the things she'd seen or heard or learned.

Her response wouldn't have worried him if they hadn't already been through so much that week. If she wanted to keep something to herself, that was fine, but she always told him when she was doing that. She said those things were for her. She would have said something else, like "I don't want to talk about it."

But Sayra didn't say what happened that day was for her alone. She wasn't just keeping something for herself; she didn't want *him* to know she was keeping something secret.

"What about you? How was your day?" she asked.

"It was good," he said. "It felt good to get out of the place, even for just a bit."

Carl noticed she didn't react to the idea of needing to get out of the apartment. Was that a question, somewhere crinkled into her brow? Had he misspoke?

"I stopped by the lake before I came home," he added. "It was quiet."

She sat back in her chair and took a drink from the bottle of soda they were sharing. "I'm surprised. Usually the leaf peepers are all over the place this time of year."

"Probably out east already, jamming up traffic in the mountains."

She chuckled.

Something was definitely wrong.

Since Carl had made dinner, Sayra offered to clean up. That was fairly normal, but again, he was taken aback. She'd been in bed for practically a week straight, ignoring calls from family, friends, and coworkers alike. She'd barely spoken to him. This evening, she was eating with him, laughing, and volunteering to help around the apartment.

Carl heard Sayra turn on the speaker in the kitchen. She asked it to play music by LyttleCafé, and the apartment was filled with the dulcet sounds of Ella Caby and her nylon 6 string. A classic. One of Sayra's favorites. It was like she was back to her old self.

Carl went into the kitchen under the pretense of getting a bottle of water, keen to check on his wife again. She gave him a kiss on the cheek as he passed by her in the narrow kitchen, humming along to Ella's latest album as he left.

He set the bottle down and went to the restroom. While he sat on the toilet, he ran a quick search for rapid recoveries from psychological trauma and post miscarriage depression.

Nothing gave him any answers. He was probably searching for the wrong things, but what was he supposed to call whatever *this* was?

It was getting late. Carl washed up, groaning at how the mirror revealed dark circles under his eyes, and ran some floss through his teeth. As he threw it away, he caught sight of something in the trash—an unusual shape next to the usual mess. It was a small black box with a logo across one side: *Recollections LLC.*

Carl's stomach dropped. He picked the box out of the trash and ran numb fingers along the edge. A small flash drive—a black shard made to fit into the port in most personal readers—was housed in it. He pushed it into the slot on the side of his head and the Recollections logo appeared on his lens. Red text appeared over his view of the restroom wall. Below it was a file titled *RBC-Patient_Report-108E2L.*

He opened it, and paragraphs of red text streamed across his view of the bathroom wall.

Carl ejected the flash and threw it back into the trash. He stood there for a moment, breathing slowly, listening to Sayra's music muffled through the door.

A lone guitar plucking. A woman's voice rising and falling with the chorus.

When the songs changed, he went back to the kitchen and poured himself a glass of whiskey.

"Really?" Sayra asked, mirth in her voice.

"Water didn't quite hit the spot," he said, which wasn't entirely untrue.

The whiskey tasted bitter after having just brushed his teeth. His gums stung from the alcohol.

Sayra knew something was wrong. The way Carl spoke to her so delicately, treating her like she was about to break, was unnerving.

After she was done with the dishes, Sayra stayed in the kitchen a moment longer, staring at the arrangement of still-drying plates, pots, and utensils while she skimmed through old messages saved to her lens. Red text rolled across her field of vision—weeks-old messages between Carl and herself. She was looking for answers, knowing she probably wouldn't like what she found, but not quite ready to fish through the trash. She didn't need the full picture, just a better idea of what had put her husband so off-balance.

She had deleted most of her recent messages, probably not by accident. Those that remained were simple, like Carl asking if she needed anything or telling her that a shower would help her feel better. At some point, he seemed to have given up with words and sent cat videos. They were adorable, but unhelpful.

Sayra tried the obituaries next, wondering if somebody had died, but she didn't recognize any of the names listed. She checked her bank account to see if she'd suddenly lost some money, but again, there was nothing out of the ordinary.

She wasn't looking in the right places, but she didn't know where to check next. Besides that, Sayra had enough trust in herself to know she would not have removed a memory on a whim. Perhaps she was just overthinking things. Best to move on. Let the past be the past, whatever it was, right?

Carl was on the couch nursing his whiskey and staring out through the window at the mountains beyond. Bags hung beneath his eyes. She hadn't caught that while they were eating together. He'd been so attentive, but just then, as he gazed off into the night sky, she felt as though she was finally seeing his true state of mind.

Sayra joined him on the couch and kissed him, her lips lingering on his a moment longer than usual, testing the waters. His lips curled into a slight grin, but his eyes still looked like they were off in the mountains.

The last time Carl had looked that way was when his niece died. She was only a teenager. She'd gone home, back across the lake, and got caught in a crossfire between police and some gang. A week later, Sayra and Carl were listening to her eulogy.

The wake was short. The body was hidden under a closed casket. Sayra learned from the girl's mother that it was because they had to save money on the service. The burial, the tombstone, the hosting family—it was all so expensive. However, a corpse's chrome still held value so long as it was undamaged. Whatever was under the lid of that girl's casket was a broken, disassembled young woman. Consequently, nobody wanted to show her face to the mourning family.

She knew that Carl knew that. The moment he saw the closed casket, he knew.

Sayra sat back on the couch and brought her husband's head to rest onto her chest. He lay there for a long while, the warmth of his cheek against her. She ran her fingers through his hair. Slowly. Gently. Her fingertips brushed against the chrome in his head. His hair was thinning more than she had realized, but she didn't mind. She thought that old men looked wise—which was totally unfair as far as she was concerned—but she was not afraid of age. She looked forward to growing old with Carl.

That was why they were trying for a baby, after all.

To grow old together.

As a family.

Carl lay against Sayra for a while, her arm draped over him like a weighted blanket. He could hear her heart beating steadily. He felt safe and lost all at once. He had his wife back, but she was fundamentally not the woman who woke up in his bed that morning.

Was that a bad thing? She'd barely been able to get out of bed since the miscarriage. Their child's death...it had destroyed her.

She wasn't in pain anymore. She was back to the way she was before it all went awry. So, why wasn't he happier? This was what he'd wished for, prayed for, when she was asleep.

Carl wanted another drink of whiskey, but he couldn't bear to loosen himself from Sayra's grip, so he sat still until he began to doze off. Eventually, she nudged him upright and told him they should go to bed.

Carl didn't bother to take his clothes off. He collapsed on his side of the bed and closed his eyes. He could feel Sayra's stare. She was probably confused and scared, trying to piece together what memories were taken from her. He felt sorry for her.

On the other hand, he didn't know what to say. Telling her what she'd done...that would be worse, wouldn't it? She'd removed those memories for a reason.

"I'm going to stay up a bit longer," she said. Then he heard their bedroom door close.

Sayra had never felt so alone. Not with Carl, at least. He'd been a constant in her life since they met, always eager to be at her side, and she'd tried to be the same for him. She'd imagined her marriage immune to the issues of her friends' and family's. Those that withered and grew more distant, were not like what they had. Carl wasn't always exciting, for certain. His idea of a good time was watching a show, walking around the neighborhood. Fishing in the mountains on a long weekend–even though he knew there were practically no fish left in the lake and he was legally required to release whatever he caught. But she couldn't imagine another life for herself. Carl was always there, always asking interesting questions, and always supporting her.

There was only one thing left to do.

Sayra dug through the trash. She found the case from Recollections and popped it open. A shiver ran up her spine. The flash drive was missing.

Carl had found it.

Sayra dug deeper into the bin, past the used floss and tissues, and came up with the tiny metal stick after a few minutes.

She wiped it against her jeans and slotted it in, bracing for the worst.

The next morning, Carl found Sayra asleep on the couch. He picked up his keys and put on a coat, careful not to wake her, and left the apartment. The sun had yet to rise, but as he drove into South Burlington, it crept up over the Green Mountains and reflected off the lake. Without it, the breeze cut through him like ice.

He arrived at Recollections a few minutes before the doors opened. It was a surprisingly small office set on the bottom two floors of a larger building. The base of the structure looked as old as the city, with cracks in the bricks and gaps in the mortar that kept it all together. The apartments above were new, added sometime in the last thirty years during the worst of the population boom—when refugees fled the flooded east coast.

A handful of protesters began to show up, carrying large signs, greeting each other as if they were old friends just casually meeting up at the park. They'd been at it so long that the news cycle had moved on. Those who remained were the loudest, but there were only four on the sidewalk. Perhaps more would show up as the day warmed up.

When the doors to Recollections opened, Carl still hadn't gotten out of his car. He watched traffic slowly increase as people went to work or drove to the store, and he wondered if he really wanted to do what he was planning. Rather, he didn't *want* to. He wondered if he *should*.

He wished Sayra had talked about it with him. They could have had the operation together or found another way to work through it. Whatever they decided, at least neither of them would have had to be alone.

Now he was doing the same thing to her, although it was different this time. She wouldn't even notice the change, not like he did. She'd already erased those memories.

Carl thought about putting the car into drive, but he couldn't bear another day like the previous one. He couldn't speak with Sayra as she was now. Not with all of his memories of what had happened. He was terrified of invalidating what she'd done by telling her what she'd forgotten. If she thought removing the memories was the best thing to do, maybe it was. Maybe that was what they needed: a restart.

Carl averted his eyes from the protesters as he walked into Recollections. A tech guided him into the operating room, and the doctor described the procedure. He showed Carl the chair that would remove the memories, explaining the process in detail.

After writing down Sayra's name and number in case there was an emergency, Carl answered a slew of basic questions: did he have any allergies, combat implants, malware, history of dementia in the family? He signed his name on a paper that gave Recollections immunity should something go wrong, and acknowledged that the removed memories became property of Recollections LLC and its subsidiaries. Finally, Carl described the situation and the memories he wanted removed, in as much detail as he could.

A call interrupted them. Carl looked at his phone long enough to see Sayra's name, then put it back into his pocket.

"I can wait if you need to take that," the doctor said, the lights in his visor gleaming.

"No. I'll call her back after."

"The procedure takes a few hours. The part where you're sitting in the chair and that little crown does its work is just a part of it—we also need to make sure you're able to walk back out through those doors, which is another matter. We're not just cutters. We gotta' put you back together afterward too. And—"

"It's fine," Carl said as he sat in the chair. It seemed to know he was there; the arms around his head flinched when he sat back.

Meanwhile, the doctor connected Carl to the chair via a physical jack in the side of his head and another in a port on his arm. He complained quietly about out-of-date chrome as a series of graphs appeared on a screen, his vitals, on another, Carl could see his heart beating—one hundred forty-two beats per minute—and felt his chest tightening.

White light flashed, and the doctor's eyes became red—a feed of data streaming across his lenses.

"Let's just do this," Carl said.

"Alright," the doctor said, his eyes a blur of red and blue. The lights flashed so quickly they seemed not to be flashing at all anymore as the arms moved in around Carl's head. "Tell me about your malignant memories."

Carl felt a burning heat on his scalp, and his vision was flooded with a flickering white light.

Then, nothing.

Sayra stumbled down the stairs, her head still aching from all the liquor from the night before. She tried Carl again as she worked her way down the steps, focusing hard on her boots, wincing at the sound of moving traffic.

He didn't answer. Again.

Carl was making a mistake. She would do anything to undo what had happened yesterday, but that wasn't an option. All she could do was try to stop her husband.

Sayra took the next bus to South Burlington. She tapped her foot incessantly as it looped around the long way. The woman seated beside her stared at her. Sayra stopped for a time, but resumed tapping a few minutes later.

That fucking idiot, Sayra thought to herself.

She tried calling Carl again, blinking away tears when it went straight to voicemail.

"How're you feeling?" the doctor asked. His words were rough, splitting Carl's head apart.

He leaned away from the man only to find that he was seated in a chair. It enveloped his head, arms unfolding around him as the power wound down. He knew what the device was and what it did, and a pit formed deep in his gut. He shouldn't be here.

Carl grunted in response and held a hand up to block the lights. A cable was still inserted into his arm. He tugged on it and loosed his arm from the machine with a loud click.

"You're all set, but the next twenty-four hours are crucial, Mr. Camirin. Take these pills. And do not stress yourself. Rest, and come morning, you'll feel better."

"Thanks," Carl said, slowly rising to his feet.

Sayra was in the lounge waiting for him. She looked a mess. Her outfit was the same one she'd worn the night before, her hair was in a tangle, and her eyes carried heavy bags beneath them.

She smiled when she saw him, but Carl could tell something was terribly wrong.

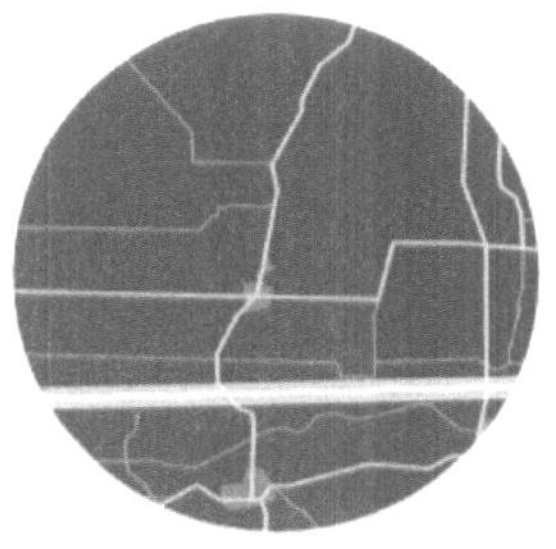

Brand New Eyes

Hemmingford, Québec — 2093

JOCELYN GLANCED INTO HER car's rear-view mirror, and golden eyes stared back at her. They still caught her off guard, even though she'd spent a month researching companies and models and colors. She'd almost chosen a heterochromatic model, like her roommate Anne-Marie had, but didn't want to seem like she was copying her. Even if Anne said it was fine.

Besides, Jocelyn liked the simplicity of her golden eyes. They stood out in the dark and reminded her of honey. She grinned back at her reflection. It felt good to like the way she looked for once.

Jocelyn touched the corner of her eye, and her expression faded. There was still a faint scar where the surgeon cut her open. Non-scarring medi-gels were available, but they weren't covered by her insurance. Neither were cozmods, like her new irises. She hadn't been able to afford the gels *and* the procedure. In another couple of months, Jocelyn could have gotten both and avoided the scarring altogether, but she wanted to get the procedure done early so she could drive herself home for the holidays.

The road was slick with snow, salt, and sand. It was an unusually cold winter, but that was always preferable to freezing rain. She tapped the brake pedal as she rounded a turn onto exit 14, all too aware of how easy it was to slip off the edge. She'd learned to drive on these roads and steered her Papa's sedan into a snowbank not far from there. She could still feel the shame and guilt from that moment, passing by that spot now. She could still hear her father exhale, and tell her it was a rite of passage, as he called a neighbor with a tow truck.

The last time Jocelyn visited home was eight years ago, before she left for university. She hadn't planned to be gone for so long, but she was busy there, and soon after found work in Toronto thanks to Anne-Marie's help. And Toronto was so much—it was hard *not* to get caught up in it.

She found it easier to stay away after her father remarried. His new wife, Sabina, always found a way to make sure she came above everything else. She was such a bitch... But it was time to go back. For at least a few days. She missed her father, the small shops, and the forests that still surrounded the town. She even missed the smell of the farms splayed out along the countryside—though she expected to be sick of it before Monday.

Hemmingford was barely a town. Blink, and it's in the rear-view. It only stretched about a kilometer from Elizabeth Road to the old cemetery, but that was part of its charm. You couldn't get those snowy forest views in Toronto, not on the city's edge, not even on the Hilton-Dean's rooftop gardens.

Jocelyn let the car park itself while she checked her lens. Red text appeared over her view of the old brick tavern in front of her: *[11:54] sorry. Presque à la porte.*

It figured Papa would be late. She'd been driving for nearly six hours, and *he* was the one running late. Sabina's kids probably kept him. Or maybe he'd just fallen asleep.

Jocelyn waited in her car, listening to the rest of the Louis Porir song she'd been playing—and then another—retreating into her coat and clinging to the car's heat. A couple left the tavern, glancing through her windshield as they walked away. It struck her how strange she must have looked alone in her (mostly) self-driving car, surrounded by beaters.

Once they'd turned their backs, Jocelyn stepped outside. Wind whipped around her hair and through her glossy silver coat. Snow crunched under her boots. She walked into the tavern quickly, keeping her eyes down, stepping where the most sand and salt had been spread. Despite that, she stumbled beside the tavern's door. Jocelyn caught herself against the wall. Her boots were better suited for city winters, with their frequent plowing and heated sidewalks. Not this mess.

[12:13] on the way, Papa said.

She found a seat at the bar and responded through her lens: *[12:13] v.*

Jocelyn fixed her hair and took off her coat. She was over-dressed for this place, where the locals came in sweatshirts and jeans and she arrived in a damn dress. The tavern's warmth rolled over her and those anxieties melted away. She turned around and stared at the real wood fireplace, surrounded by multi-colored Christmas lights. The fire crackled and popped, radiating a golden warmth from behind an iron grate. The whole building smelled of smoke and fried food and fresh-cut wreaths. It was intoxicating. It was home. For as much as she loved Toronto, Jocelyn had missed this.

She left her coat at the bar and walked over to the fire. Orange firelight danced across her dress, diluted by what rays came through the dusty windows. It felt like she was in an old picture—no—a painting. She could imagine it when she closed her eyes. A visage like the renaissance masters': a young woman against strong contrasting light, measuring something in a little scale. Any second, the angel Gabriel could have come through the windows and announced whatever it was Gabriel announced.

The daydream might have been better if she'd paid more attention in her sole art history class. Or if her imagination had picked something she wasn't so damn clueless about.

Jocelyn checked her lens again for new messages. There were none.

A few minutes passed before Jocelyn heard her name.

Her father's voice came from behind—followed shortly by the door slamming shut. His hair swept to the side and receded to his temples. Dark circles hung beneath his eyes, yet they gleamed in the mix of electric and fire light. Sabina's kids were running him ragged, Jocelyn kept telling him on their irregular calls. That, and a recent dispute over an ancient farm that he owned in Hallerton, had him stressed out.

Despite all of that, his smile still lit up the room. Just like it used to.

"Hey, Papa," Jocelyn said.

She rushed to hug him, but as she did, his body stiffened, betraying his hesitation. A wordless breath left his mouth. Jocelyn took a step back and looked up into his eyes and he recoiled under her gaze. She looked around the room. People were staring at them. No, at *her*. Was she imagining it? No. When she met the bartender's eyes, he averted them. He tried to make it look like he was just working, but the fucker was cleaning an *obviously* spotless glass.

Jocelyn stepped aside, pulling her father with her beside the door. A cold draft buffeted her face.

"What's wrong?" she asked, whispering.

"It's nothing," he said. Liar.

"Everyone is staring at me right now. What's the matter? Did I take somebody's seat or something?" She forced a laugh.

"Look, honey," Her father rubbed the back of his neck. "People here aren't used to... You know I'm pretty comfortable with whatever... But the *habitants*. Your stepmom is going to..."

"*Dis-le*," Jocelyn spat. She knew it sounded harsh as soon as she said it, but her father was muttering, and everyone was still stealing glances at her. Glaring. "Say what you're trying to say."

"I didn't know you'd changed your eyes, honey," he whispered.

Jocelyn smiled at him, her throat catching. "Anne-Marie said I should get a heterochromatic pair—a different color for each eye—but I wanted something a bit different. Simpler. You always called me *honey*. This color reminded me of that."

Her father looked like he would have preferred to jump into the Richelieu than have that conversation. Sweat formed along his brow and he clenched his hands.

"That's sweet, honey," he said, faltering on the last word.

"*Vraiment?* Because it seems like you hate them."

"I don't. It's just... I'm sorry, but I need to leave."

Jocelyn wanted to scream, but she felt as though she didn't have the air in her lungs.

"Get whatever you want to eat," he continued. "Tell Jed to put it on my tab."

"You're kidding me."

"I need to talk to Sabina."

"Your wife can fucking wait." Jocelyn felt her voice rise. She took a breath, blinked away a tear, and said, "If you won't even have lunch with me, I will get in that car and go back to Toronto right now. I'll grab takeaway and eat it on the 401. Without you. And I won't come back."

He stared down at the floor.

"*Tabarnak*," he muttered. "Things are different here. People don't get cosmetics like… *that*. These are farmers and artisans and *blood and sweat* types. Earrings and tattoos are one thing, and I'd rather somebody replace a missing leg than not, but cozmods are…"

Jocelyn's feet felt like lead. She was hungry. She did not want to get back in her car again. She didn't want to follow through. She just wanted him to say something—anything—that she could convince herself was some kind of acceptance, that said she was more than the cozmods in her eyes. That she could still call Hemmingford home.

"What was so wrong with the eyes God gave you, honey?" he asked. "You were always beautiful. You didn't need any work done."

"I think they look nice," she said. "After I got these, I felt good about myself for the first time in a *long* time when I looked into the mirror. I was excited to show you them. But mostly, I just wanted to have lunch with my father."

He stared back at her. If he felt any guilt or defiance, she couldn't see it. He just looked like he wanted to escape.

"Goodbye, Papa," Jocelyn said.

She left the old tavern.

It was only in the Timmy's drive-thru that she realized she'd left her coat behind in the orange light of the fireplace.

Buying Time

Portland, Maine — 2107

THE FURNACE GLOWED MOLTEN red as white-hot flames danced around inside. A glass orb was suspended on the end of a blowpipe, its surface malleable and uncertain. The heatsink embedded in my forearm hummed. Metal shifted and coolant flowed like blood, emitting pale blue light and siphoning the furnace's sweltering breath. Even with the mod, my brow and arms shone with sweat.

I took a deep breath.

Pull the glass from the furnace. Spin the blowpipe. Dab the end in shards of colored glass. Spin to gather them around the base of the molten orb. Back into the furnace to melt it in with the rest of the piece, always spinning the pipe. Every second, every movement affected the strength and make of the bauble.

By the time I'd severed the glass from the blowpipe and taken it to the kiln, I couldn't help but notice that Ian was already blowing his third piece for the day. That was just my first. I watched him work for a moment, how the heat bent around the heat shields implanted in his face and forearms—black strips along the bridge of his nose, cheeks, and arm. There was barely a bead of sweat on his brow. There was also much less skin for him to sweat through. Perhaps that was the new model's secret.

The Atlantic Glass Studio subsidized installations that would improve production, but I couldn't afford even their discounted rate or the contract that came with it. Besides, in exchange for the deal, they wanted a commitment from the employee that they would remain at the company for five years, minimum. Corporate waved off the clause like it was nothing. After all, plenty of other companies did the same thing. "Cephas Gold put seven years on their contracts," Ian said after his surgery, like a goddamn parrot.

AGS cut me a special deal for an outdated model then patted themselves on the back for it as though they were saints. All it cost was a small percentage of my wages for three years. One more and I'd earn out. Soon, I would own the rights to my left arm again.

I returned to the furnace, sweating, and began reheating the blowpipe for a new gather. Just as I was about to put it into the furnace, my phone rang. I checked it, curious. Everyone I knew texted. It was Mom. Ian took the blowpipe for me while I answered it. He was a sell-out, but not a bad guy. I guess.

Grandpa Clark was dead. It wasn't a shock. He'd lived a long seventy-eight years and had been ill lately. Still, the numbness that followed Mom's words was...

I took Thursday off work and made the drive to Skowhegan. The weather was decent, but the roads up north weren't cleared as well as those around the city. I wasn't able to get my car's snows on that year, so instead I relied on some old all-seasons and a back-road prayer. When I arrived at my mother's house, every muscle in my neck ached.

The eulogy my mother gave was conflicted. She spoke about how proud Grandpa was to have protected his family and how—privately—he was ashamed of his deeds overseas. When I asked her about it later she said, "He never spoke about it, but I could tell. The war changed him."

I suppose I had to take her word for it. I was too young to remember what Grandpa was like before he shipped off, and the only pictures from his youth were analog—paper stained by age and more floods than I could remember. Mom saved a few of them digitally, but the scans were from old machines and became grainy whenever I zoomed in.

Grandpa Clark didn't leave anything to me, but my mother wound up in possession of an old pocket watch. I'd seen the old man wearing it before. It never left his side, but I never thought much of the antique. It was as common a sight as the old man's *Tortured Poets* tee and vague complaints about how the new generation was taking the country in the wrong direction. Comments which were inevitably followed up by phrases like, "Back in my day..."

Before I left Skowhegan, Mom gave me the pocket watch. Like all good hand-me-downs, it came with a lecture told beneath a yellow light in her kitchen. I listened with a hot mug of cocoa between my hands, doctored with a bit of maple syrup. The real stuff. The kind I remembered growing up with. It was just as abundant in Portland, but they called it *liquid gold* for a reason.

The watch was made by a distant relative in Québec City when it was under British rule. It had been a gift for an equally distant grandmother, which seemed like an odd gift for a woman during those times. That long ago—I'm pretty sure—only men wore watches. That was why women got wed, so they could bring something around to tell time. Clingy little timepieces.

"That really happened?" I asked.

"Your Grandpa had lots of stories. A weird amount of them involved that damn watch." Mom laughed. "He said that it got him a sales job in the city back in the 50s. He 'sold' it to the manager. Told him a tale about how it was handmade, accurate to a tee, all kinds of things. I'm sure some of them were actually true."

In a moment of silence, a gust of wind shook the old house.

Mom continued. "He said that watch saved him in the war, more so than any of the gear they equipped him with. He never elaborated. I think it just reminded him of home. Going through what he did, I think a reminder of what he fought for helped him get through it."

The antique had been in the family since then, whether or not the British-Canadian woman accepted the gift. Clearly somebody had. Mom and I tried to debunk the old tale over a second mug of cocoa. Neither of us could, though neither of us tried that hard. It was just nice to have a mystery and to be back home for a little while.

Damn.

I missed the old man.

The antique lived on my desk for the next month, collecting dust while I listened to arguments arising from the antique shop below my floorboards. I wasn't sure what to do with the old thing. It made me wish I'd spent more time with Grandpa. He and Grandma seemed like fine people, but they had lived all the way up in Eagle Lake. It was hard to find time to make the trek. Now they were both gone.

I tried carrying the old pocket watch around for a while. It felt strange to have that weight hanging from me, especially when I could just check the time on my phone or lens. So, it went back onto the desk.

It was a good conversation piece, if nothing else. It fascinated a girl, Emily, who came over one evening. I recounted what I knew, and she seemed to like my grandfather's old stories. I never heard from her after that. Never found out why.

I popped a tire while driving to work that spring. The snow had melted, mostly, but there was still plenty of mud to slide around on. Plenty of potholes. The towing company brought my car to Nicky's. She wouldn't nickel and dime me, but the final bill was still too much: a full month's rent. Still, I paid it. What other choice did I have? I couldn't walk to work. Portland's bus garage had shut down five years ago.

"You've got to keep an eye on that engine, too," Nicky said before I left her garage. "It's fine for now, but it's not looking good."

"Will it get me into town and back?"

"For now, sure, but I wouldn't count on it to pass inspection next year."

I sucked in a breath. "Call me if you can offer me something cheap before then?"

"You and everyone else with these old burners. We're just as starved for parts as you are for fuel." Then, more gently, she added, "I'll do what I can, but you know how it is. Everyone driving these antiques are doing so for a reason, and the suits are phasing all this old tech out. Already got rid of them in the big cities. You watch, in a few years, the only place you'll find these fossil foamers is a car show or some rich prick's garage."

"Probably." I forced a smile. "Thanks, Nicky."

The car got me to work the next day and the day after that. It didn't seem any worse off than it did before the popped tire, but Nicky was an old friend. She wouldn't lie about something like that. I'd always known the car wouldn't last, but replacing it felt impossible. I could always get a cab to work, but that would cost more than a car after a while.

There was also the issue of rent. I'd already eaten into that fund with the new tire and groceries. Offsetting that with instant ramen dinners helped, but only so much. I would have killed for a decent burger.

An orb of molten glass spun on the end of my blowpipe and I rolled it across the marvel, using the metal surface to shape and cool it just enough. Bands of glass formed abstract ribbons within the piece. It was coming along well, but it was taking so long to form. Too long. Fucking Ian was on break, reading something on his tablet. Imagine having the time to take a full break.

After work, I walked to the antique shop below my apartment. It was all I could think of. If executives and tourists were willing to buy glass baubles that did nothing, surely they would pay a few pennies for an antique watch. I didn't want to sell it, but it was either that or find a new place to live. I suppose I could have robbed a bank, but I was pretty sure I didn't have that in me. I didn't have enough closet space for that much hard cash, either.

"Well, isn't this a surprise," the shopkeeper said when I walked in the door. He put aside an old brass contraption and wiped his hands off on a rag, streaking black oil stains across it.

"Hey, Mr. Suero." A bell clattered behind me as I stepped forward.

"I don't see any baked goods from your mother, so you must be here on business. You were never one to swing by for a chat. What can I do for you?"

"Should've been a detective, sir," I said as I retrieved the watch from my pocket.

"By God," Mr. Suero said. He adjusted his glasses and took the watch into work-stained hands, cradling it as if it were a tiny robin's egg. I followed him. My throat felt dry. He prodded at the watch gently, like it could break at any moment, and I worried I might have damaged it carrying it around earlier that year.

"It's worth something?" I asked. A part of me hoped it wasn't.

Mr. Suero glanced between the watch and me, collected himself, and took on the air of a historian. "It's got a Smith & Son face, but the body is something totally different. Normally, that would devalue it, but the construction is exquisite. It's also in good shape, save for a few scratches, but I think I could get rid of those. Or at least make them harder to see." He giggled. "The case is gold, maybe twelve karat? I'll have to check again to be sure. If you open up the back..."

He exposed the back of the watch. Rings of gears, ribbons of wire and glass, whirled around the center. They were constantly spinning back and forth. With every rotation, a mechanism behind it shifted in slight, precise movements. It was constant and mesmerizing.

"This is a tourbillon, invented by Abraham-Louis Breguet in the... 19th century, I believe. Quite rare, and surprising to find it on an independently made piece."

"It's stunning."

"It is, isn't it?"

I wanted to keep it. In a few seconds, Mr. Suero had shown me the beauty hidden in that unassuming watch. But that wasn't an option. "How much?"

"I can take it off your hands for a few thousand," he said.

My gut dropped.

He held up a finger. "That's just what I'm able to part with right now. Considering you're looking to get rid of this beaut, I imagine doing so *right now* is key. I would recommend you find somebody to appraise this. Somebody who knows more about watches. Between the gold and the tourbillon, you could be looking at much more, if you can afford the delay."

It was tempting, but rent was coming up so soon.

"Do you know anyone who could look at it?"

"Sure. I have a friend in New York who could give you a better sense of its worth. She's away right now, but she should be around in a few months, I think."

"I can't wait that long."

Mr. Suero set the watch down. "I see."

He was quiet for a moment, running his fingers through the thin white beard on his chin.

"I can offer you twenty-five hundred. For now. That should help hold you over. Then, I'll contact my friend in New York and get it appraised. Once I have a better idea of the value and find a buyer, you can have... You can have forty percent of whatever it sells for. I'll pay for the appraisal and shipping out of my cut. How does that sound?"

"Forty percent?"

He smiled. "Appraisal and finding a legit buyer will take some time and resources. You won't need to worry about that. And if I'm right, you'll walk away with much more than what I can give you today with no effort on your part." He grinned. "*And,* I won't tell your mother about this."

Mr. Suero reached his hand out. I felt my stomach turn. But I took it. What other choice did I have?

"Four-thousand up front, and you have a deal."

"I told you, that's more than I can do right now." Mr. Suero put his hand into his pocket. "I'm not trying to hustle you, son, but I have to make rent too."

I nodded. Still, I needed more than twenty-five hundred to keep the lights on.

"Three?" I asked.

Mr. Suero pursed his lips and glanced down at the watch. "I'll do twenty-eight hundred. No higher."

It wasn't ideal, but it would have to do.

"Deal."

The next few months were difficult but uneventful. I checked in with Mr. Suero every few weeks. He didn't get the watch appraised until mid-spring. It took longer to find a buyer, but when he did, he came knocking on my door. Mr. Suero transferred my cut and a number appeared in red on my lens. I had to sit down.

"More than you expected? Good. Quit that job of yours and go and tour the country, or whatever's left of it. Or move out of this dump, get yourself a real house. Maybe something in the 'burbs. I think that's what I'll do."

I nodded. I could have done any of that with the money. It wasn't a fortune, but it was plenty to get a new car and make a new life for myself. But I'd only ever known Maine—Skowhegan, Portland, and the little towns around it. My mother was still here, and my grandparent's graves. Even quitting my job was difficult to grapple with. My arm, the heat sink humming quietly even then, was made for glassblowing. That's what I was—and not even the small fortune that Mr. Suero delivered would make me into something else.

"Fuck," I whispered.

Atlantic Essentials

Punta Loyola, Argentina — 2121

HERNÁN LICKED HIS CHAPPED lips and tasted blood. He untied his boots by the apartment door, then searched a drawer for a stick of lip balm. He gave himself a thick coat, then capped and tucked it away in his pocket for the next day.

Frances sat at the dining table, thin fingertips supporting her head, the surface before her a mess of screens and paper. Envelopes, torn apart, formed a partial ring around her chair. When she shifted her weight, it wobbled, one leg shorter than the rest. She glanced up at him, attempted a smile, and said, "Rent went up again."

Again.

The word twisted in Hernán's gut. He was already working overtime at the port whenever he could. Frances spent most of her time with their son so they wouldn't have to pay for childcare. She used to work at the school full time—lately, she helped as a substitute as needed—but she'd gone without a raise for years and had started with low pay to begin with. These days, it felt like she was donating her time, using the school to escape their small apartment for a few hours each week. They had looked for something else, but there were few options in Punta Loyola.

The small town served as a major port for the Antarctic ice market, which was becoming more integrated into the world as other sources of fresh water dried out or became contaminated. Ice came to Punta Loyola, then went to the rest of South America, and the money went straight to a bunch of Americano suits. They kicked a bit of the wealth toward their employees, at least. Hernán was pretty sure it was thanks to some labor law they couldn't squirm out of, but regardless, it was the best paying job most people could get in town. His wages had risen slightly each year. Barely. Last December his wage increased an extra three hundred pesos per hour—barely a dollar in the Estados Unidos.

It was better than nothing, he supposed.

Frances had been busy crunching numbers. The bags under her eyes suggested she'd been at it for a while. She'd scrawled lists and equations onto no less than four notepads, and her tablet displayed a spreadsheet filled with numbers in black and red. He couldn't see them all from where he stood, but the ratio skewed too far in the red.

"Is Mateo asleep?" Hernán asked. It had been a long day. Before he got into that with Frances, he wanted to check on their son.

She shrugged. "He's supposed to be. Probably isn't."

"I'm going to check on him," Hernán whispered. When Frances rolled her eyes at him, he kissed her forehead.

Mateo was in his purple pajamas, sitting up in bed holding a picture book: *Amadeo y el Gigante Antártico*. It looked massive in his little hands. He balanced it against his knee and held a flashlight up to the pages, even though he couldn't read that one without help. Frances insisted he had a better grasp for reading than most three-year-old boys. Unfortunately, that only encouraged him to pick up books like *Amadeo* then became frustrated about how hard they were to read. However, that evening, he seemed content to look at the pictures. Mateo's dark brown eyes scanned them in rapt attention, olive fingers tracing the pages. He hadn't even noticed he'd been caught.

Hernán tapped on the open door. Mateo's eyes shot up to meet his.

"Papá!" Mateo tried to throw off his covers, but he only became more tangled in them. He stumbled out of his old racecar-shaped bed, knocking his knee against the frame, and still landed on both feet. Hernán didn't have time to ask if he was alright before his son crashed into him. His weight—it was always more than Hernán expected—nearly knocked him off his feet. Hernán made a show of his stumble. He swung around, planted his feet, picked up Mateo, and spun him around. Mateo held on tight. His fingers dug into Hernán's arm. Then the boy fought back with all his strength.

Hernán lifted his son above his head and threatened to put him up on the shelf and leave him there. Mateo said his lines—Amadeo's words verbatim from the book—and wrestled Hernán with a renewed strength. Hernán let himself fall, as gently as he could, to his knees. Mateo pressed his wrists into the floor, pinning him. However, he seemed to forget that he had to *keep* his papá's arms pinned. Mateo gave a defiant roar and raised his fists in sweet victory. Hernán, his wrists freed, took the opportunity to pick the boy up and throw Mateo back into his racecar bed. The boy landed hard enough that he bounced back up, giggling. Then, like a puma, he leapt onto Hernán's shoulders.

Frances cleared her throat and Hernán spun to face her. Something popped in his back.

"*Silencio*," Frances hissed. "What will the neighbors say if they hear you throwing Mateo around the room—at this hour, no less?"

"I'll go to sleep if you read this to me, Papá," Mateo said, jumping back into his bed and holding up the book.

"We read that earlier today, mijo," Frances said.

"Papá, you can start on page five," Mateo said. "I already read the pictures on the other pages."

"He's wound himself up now," Hernán said to her, stretching his back.

"*You* wound him up," Frances said.

"Ah, nothing to be done about it. Besides, it's a short book." Then, to Mateo, he said, "Get in bed. Hurry, before Mamá can say no. And you had better sleep after this. Otherwise, we're both in trouble."

The pain meds were in the kitchen, next to the liquor. There weren't many left. Hernán took two to help ease whatever muscle had pulled and hoped that was all he would need. If he had to miss his shift the following day, he wouldn't get those hours back.

He joined Frances at the table and asked, "How bad is it this time?"

"The super wants another ten thousand pesos each month."

Hernán stood back up from the table and poured a drink. There wasn't much pisco left, and they were out of ice again. He watched the amber wine collapse into the glass and thought about how many extra hours he would have to work to make up the increase. It wasn't as bad as last time, but he was already stretched thin. They both were.

"You shouldn't drink," Frances said. "Not with the pill you just had."

"It's not for me," he said, placing the glass in front of her. She considered it for a moment, then took it in one long drink.

"Thanks," she said, then pushed the empty glass aside. "I'm sorry, but we need you to put in more time at the port. I don't see another way. We can only cut back so much before we start starving ourselves, and I can't take on any more hours at the school. There are only so many favors I can cash in before I need to send Mateo to the day care in Río Gallegos, and they are expensive. If he's even approved."

"I'm not sure that I can do more hours," Hernán said. "It's cheaper to bring on new part-timers than pay my wage. The company's over-staffed, and I doubt it's an accident. I'll keep checking the schedule and signing up where I can, but there are only so many extra hours to go round. It's becoming competitive in a way that I don't like."

"What do you mean?"

He shrugged. "Everyone's being polite about their overtime for now, but what will happen in a few weeks? We're not the only ones crunching numbers tonight. I can name at least half a dozen people in this very building who I work with. I'm sure the super's given each of them an increase too."

"You hear anything from them about this?"

"Nah. Only one I know well is Flick, and he's always tight-lipped about money. Most he's said is a warning: 'Don't take too much extra time.' Something about Isabella and her schedule. She was taking a lot of the extra hours, cutting the line to put her name in early, and she just got fired. Officially, she was stealing ice from the warehouse, but Flick says there's more to it. He said, 'They wanted to get rid of an overpaid asset.'"

"You think he's right?"

"I don't know. Flick can be a bit paranoid, but I wouldn't be surprised. You know how the Americanos are—always cutting costs in the name of their God: year-over-year growth."

"How many Americanos do you know, again?"

"Three. But come on, you can't say I'm wrong."

Frances got up from the table and refilled her glass.

Hernán asked, "Where are we right now, if nothing changes? No extra overtime. No loss."

"Then we can almost afford this apartment," she said.

"Okay. How long would we have before the super puts an eviction notice on our door?"

When she rejoined him at the table, Hernán stole her glass and took a sip. The wine had a fruity aftertaste that clung to his tongue. Frances shot him a look that read, *you shouldn't have done that.*

She took the glass back then showed him the tablet. He picked it up, scanning the color-coded cells and numbers. It didn't instill him with hope, but at a glance, it didn't seem as bad as he feared.

Frances said, "Even if we make a few more concessions, we're still short nearly two hundred pesos. That means cooking at home all the time, buying in bulk where possible, cutting the internet—we can use the café's—basically, no more spending on anything that is not absolutely essential. Rent, food, water, you understand. We can make up some of the difference by selling a few things we don't need, although there's not much left that we can pawn. There are a few welfare programs we can apply for that will help too, but not many. The most impactful ones aren't easily accessible this far from Buenos Aires."

Hernán considered the possibilities, starting with the worst-case scenario: they couldn't find the money. They wouldn't be able to stay, that was for certain. The ideal result was to move to a new place in Punta Loyola or neighboring Río Gallegos. But there were few options in the former, and all were owned by Pepsi-Pata. The company ensured that rent was about the same no matter which building you looked at. As for the latter, Río Gallegos was even more expensive. That was where the suits lived.

Hernán's family came from Chile, but he hadn't spoken to them in some time and wasn't eager to look for handouts there. His siblings were all dealing with their own troubles, last he heard. He wasn't sure that they could help, and he didn't want to further stress any of them.

Frances had family in Noroeste Argentino who they could probably stay with for a while. They were good people, overall. A bit nosy, but he could put up with that for a roof over his family's head. It wouldn't be difficult to get a job in the lithium mines near them, but he'd rather avoid that if possible. It seemed as though every month or two there was news of management issues, broken equipment, collapsed shafts, and lost or dead miners. And that was just the news that went public. He shuddered to imagine what might be swept under the rug.

Besides, Hernán liked moving ice. Operating a forklift wasn't particularly thrilling work, but he liked the idea that he was helping provide fresh water to the world. He was a cog in the machine either way, but at least the ice machine felt more useful.

"I might be able to make up the pesos," Hernán said, "but I won't have it every week. Depends on the purchases people up north are making, how many fishermen come through, and if a storm gets in the way that could mean one week I don't even get my normal hours. You know how it is."

"And we need to account for winter," Frances added, "for when the ice shipments stop altogether. We can't afford that cut in your hours this year, and nothing else here will make up the difference. Even if I take on more hours at the school."

"For now, I will just keep taking the extra shifts that I can. We can figure out the details later."

"We really can't." Frances sighed, cradling her head in her hands. "For a while, you're right, but we don't have a lot saved. We don't have much to pawn. And you said yourself that your hours are unpredictable. Mine are too. Unless that changes—or the the company finally decides to pay its staff decent wages—it's just going to slow the process. We still need to find a *solution*, ideally one that doesn't end with us moving into a shelter or having to leave town. It was hard enough for us to find work in the first place—I don't want to go through that again."

"We'll find a way." Hernán took her hand. "You and I always do."

"We don't have long to find it," she whispered, her eyes lingering on the door to Mateo's room.

The next day, two ships were scheduled to arrive before noon. Hernán was at the Pepsi-Pata warehouse, in a forklift, by five in the morning. Bricks of Antarctic ice filled the building. The prior day's shipment had filled the shelves and forced them to set the rest in the halls. There was nowhere else to put the ice.

Hernán's breath misted in the air. He took the lip balm from his pocket and applied a heavy coat. There was little they could do until the first ship arrived, so Hernán sought out Flick. The American was easy to find thanks to the New Miami Marlins' logo sewn onto the back of his jacket.

Flick was near his forklift, which he'd parked near a side entrance where a few office staff spoke amongst themselves in English, sometimes glancing at the columns of ice, sometimes taking on blank stares as they peered at something through their lenses. A video call, probably, but for all they knew, Señor Aquino may as well have been playing solitaire. It wouldn't have been the first time.

"I think they're trying to decide what to do with the excess ice," Flick said as Hernán approached. "Word is, the northbound ship we're loading isn't coming in fresh. Won't be able to fit a full load on it, so we might not have room to store everything after today's ice gets dropped off." Flick clicked his tongue. "They don't pay us enough as it is. Least they could do is give us a bag or two. Let us take it off their hands for a change."

"They know you would just use it to chill your whiskey." Hernán grinned.

"Listen, Americans love donating to charity. I'll declare my-self an alcoholic and tell them I need to chill my medicine. Señor Aquino will double over to write it off on his taxes."

"Yeah, that should work. Go let *el jefe* know about your condition."

Flick pursed his lips. "Nah. I'd like to keep my job, thanks."

Banners of gold and red hung over the Atlantic Ocean, herald-ing the rising sun. The ever-present odor of salt and fish clung to the air. The coast was as flat as the ocean was still. Even after all his years in Argentina, it still felt odd not to see a single mountain or even the suggestion of a hill. Everything was just scrubland as far as the eye could see. Even the buildings seemed small compared to what he grew up around in Santiago. The town of Punta Loyola offered a couple of apartment buildings standing four or five stories tall, but no more. From the port, he could barely make out their silhouettes against dawn's sky.

Hernán, driving alongside Flick's lift and two dozen others, transported a brick of ice toward the first ship of the day: Maersk Lisboa. It was an old vessel that could carry up to 16,000 shipping containers. Those on its current voyage were modified to keep the ice in tact, and retain any water that melt-ed. Because of that, the containers they slid the ice into were thicker than most, so it could only carry about 15,000 of them.

It carried less than that, however, since it was already loaded with a few thousand dry containers. A few would get unloaded there—goods for Punta Loyola and Río Gallegos—but most of it was bound for other, larger ports.

From Punta Loyola, the ship would transport ice to Uruguay, Brazil, and French Guiana before taking a new cargo of meat, spices, and textiles to North America and Europe, manufactured goods to Africa, raw materials to South America, and so on—making up the Atlantic Essentials trade route. It had always been an important system, made even more so with the addition of the ice trade.

Maersk Lisboa began its journey north just as the second ship arrived. It was a massive icebreaker full of similarly insulated containers. Each carried blocks of ice from Belgrano III, a cutting station on the Antarctic shore. As the vessel docked, one of the office managers spoke through an old megaphone in broken Spanish, her voice carried across the coast: "El Yermak atracado. Transfiera todo hielo al lugar al... Almacenamiento." Then, this time in fluent English, "The Yermak's docked. Move all of the ice aboard it into the warehouse, please!"

Their fleet of forklifts converged on the icebreaker in unison, before she finished instructing them. As they approached the Yermak, her crew began lowering a ramp.

The Yermak's shipment fit in the warehouse, but it forced most of the forklifts to park outside, as their usual spots in the garage were taken by ice. Maybe the company would finally build a second warehouse when Señor Aquino saw them all parked outside. Probably not, but one could hope.

Hernán parked near the office and hurried inside to check the next few days' schedule. He needed to get there quickly so he could sign up for overtime. However, nearly a dozen others beat him to it. They wrote directly on the calendar, signing their name on days that required additional staff. Flick already was among the crowd. He made an opening for Hernán, which he took gratefully, pushing up to the Calendar and picking up a pen.

Next week was a slow one. A shipment would arrive from Cape Town on Sunday, probably carrying platinum and other metals. Another Maersk vessel was coming that day too, taking some of their ice away. Everyone on staff was required to show up for those vessels.

In the two days before then, use of the dock was being rented out to some large fishing boats, with half a dozen spaces below each day on the calendar for volunteers to work overtime to help move their cargo. They were already taken. Flick had his name on both. His writing was jagged, sharp as daggers.

Hernán signed his name at the bottom of the calendar, marking himself as available to sub in for anyone should they call in sick, or fail to show up. It wasn't impossible, but Hernán would need a miracle to see any overtime that week.

"I tried to save you a space," Flick said, "but Louisa was too quick for me."

"It's okay," Hernán lied. He put the pen down and stepped away from the calendar so others could sign up for the substitution slots. He could sense the disappointment radiating off everyone who arrived after him.

"If I get sick or something, I won't call in. I'll call you instead. Just show up."

"Gracias," Hernán said. Then, to prove he was fine with Flick taking the last overtime slots, he said, "Hey, why don't you and Jhonny come by the apartment this evening? It's been a while."

Flick looked just as surprised as Hernán felt. They hadn't gotten together much lately, and Hernán hadn't planned to on account of their financial situation. Even small gatherings like that were unaffordable. Frances was going to hate him for it, but he couldn't exactly tell Flick that anymore.

"Sure," Flick said. "Is five good?"

"Yeah, five is good."

Hernán stayed behind as the hall cleared out. In a few minutes, the office building was silent—save for the gentle typing that came from the room just across the hall. He eyed the calendar full of signatures. His wasn't where it mattered. Most of the staff hadn't gotten overtime, and nobody who managed to sign up would miss the fishing boats tomorrow or Saturday. Even if somebody did call in, management was just as likely to call Hernán as they were anyone else on the crew.

Hernán needed to talk to Señor Aquino. Jefe probably wouldn't do anything to help. Even if he wanted to, which was unlikely, it wasn't as if the man could conjure an additional ship at port. Did that matter, though? Whether or not it was realistic, Hernán couldn't afford not to try. Missing one week's overtime was bad enough. If things kept on that way, he and Frances would start missing rent.

Hernán walked into the main office. It was brightly lit and occupied by three managers, all with their desks mostly empty. Hernán was never sure why they needed three managers, but he smiled at them each nonetheless, trying to come off as pleasantly as he could. If he could just win over one, perhaps he stood a chance.

The three leaned back in their seats, almost in unison. One of their chairs emitted a squeak. Blue and red lights faded from their eyes as their lenses turned off. Señor Aquino drank from a mug. "Lunes" was written on it in a blood-red font that looked like it belonged in an ad for a horror film.

"Sorry to bother you all," Hernán said, focusing on speaking English as clearly as he could. He spoke it well, but with all three of them focused on him, it suddenly didn't seem so easy. Señor Aquino—the one whose decisions actually mattered—was from New York. He tended to react better when he didn't have to communicate in Spanish. His Spanish was awful. "But I would appreciate a moment of your time, if you don't mind."

Señor Aquino gestured toward him and took another drink. *Go on*, the Americano suggested, glaring at Hernán from over the rim of his mug.

Hernán explained the rising cost of rent, of living, of making sure there was food and water at the table for his wife and child, and hoped that the man could relate to any part of his troubles. The three displayed a full spectrum of reactions. On his right, Miguel turned back to his work. Best-case scenario, he may have simply recognized that his opinion wouldn't change anyone's mind. He was the newest of the three, after all. Worst case, he was signaling to the others not to waste their time.

On Hernán's left, Emilia—the woman who'd announced the Yermak earlier—seemed engrossed by his story. She let her computer screen blacken as her attention became solely focused on him. She was American as well, though her accent was completely different than Señor Aquino's. It was much more drawn-out, almost like she slurred some of her words.

Between them, Señor Aquino didn't seem disinterested, but his expression could have meant anything. Lines formed along his brow and a light flickered on his lens as he peered at something Hernán couldn't see. Was he trying to verify Hernán's claims, or contacting somebody in the Estados Unidos? Or was he just bored and feigning politeness? Hernán spoke his piece anyway, trying to discern something—anything—from Señor Aquino's flickering red eyes.

"How much time do you have?" Emilia asked about the impending eviction he'd described.

"If things remain as they are, a month. Maybe two." He was stretching the truth a bit. He and Frances probably had three or four months, but they would need to start looking for work and a new place to live sooner than that if nothing changed.

The lights in Señor Aquino's eyes dimmed. "You're not the only one in this situation. The cost of living here is awful. We all feel it. Be glad you have one of the company residencies, those are subsidized by Pepsi-Pata." He shrugged. "I can't remove anyone from the schedule because you're the one who thought to come talk to us. The company won't let me over-staff those extra days, either. But if anyone doesn't show—and you're here—you can take their spot."

"My work anniversary is coming up soon," Hernán said. "Perhaps we could have my evaluation early? Even a small raise would—"

"Can't do that, sorry," Señor Aquino cut him off. "If I let you cut in line, everyone will try the same, and the company will be all over my ass."

"I understand. I will be ready to work then, if you need more help this week."

"Sí," Emilia said, smiling. "Hang close by. You never know when you'll be needed around here. The weather makes shipping so unpredictable."

"Thank you." Hernán bit his tongue, wondering why he'd ever thought the suits would help.

Although she'd spent the last hour berating Hernán, Frances became the perfect hostess once Flick and his husband arrived. She took Jhon's coat and thanked Flick for bringing a bottle of whiskey—ignoring that it was already half drunk—and offered the charcuterie board she'd made from scraps in their fridge. Jhon asked about one of her cheeses while Hernán poured drinks. Flick took over for him, practically robbing the bottle from Hernán's hand. He recalled his days bartending and made a show of how he flipped the glasses around. Things were bad for all of them, and the gathering should never have happened, but Hernán was glad they could all still enjoy the moment anyway.

Mateo entertained their guests as well, telling stories as if he'd been the main character, though Hernán recognized each story from the books they read together. When somebody asked him a question about the tale, he made something up.

Each addition became more exceptional than the last, until Mateo was acting out a whole fight scene, playing the part of all seventeen ninjas, throwing ninja stars (bottle caps) around the room. Frances put an end to that after one struck her forehead. Flick complimented Mateo's aim after she'd turned her back, and the boy's shame curled into a mischievous, toothy grin.

After they drained what remained of Flick's whiskey, Hernán shared the bottle of pisco. Flick was the first to pour himself a glass. When Hernán suggested that he slow down, Flick repeated his line about making himself a charity case to the Americanos.

"It's got to be *convincente*," he said, lips pressed to the edge of his glass.

Flick shifted clumsily between English and Spanish as the evening continued, his arms animated and his eyes wide. The next time he held up an empty glass Hernán took it into the kitchen. Frances excused herself and followed him.

"Is something wrong with Flick?" Frances asked quietly. "I've never seen him so—"

"Anything I can help with over there?" Jhon called out to them.

Flick roared and chased Mateo. The child couldn't stop giggling. It was impossible to tell if the way Flick stumbled into the walls was part of the game or not. Something thudded on the ground and Jhon gave a short laugh before running over to pick whatever it was up, chastising the boys in hushed tones.

"Just make sure your man doesn't break anything I can't fix," Frances shouted to Jhon.

Jhon made an uncertain grunting sound in response.

"Plenty's wrong," Hernán whispered to Frances, pouring a new drink for Flick and topping off her glass. He felt like she was too close—like the walls were closing in. Theirs was a tiny, God-forsaken kitchen. "But I'm taking care of it as best I can."

"No es cuidar la situación. How does this help?"

Hernán opened his mouth to explain, but he couldn't find the words.

Frances frowned, glanced back at Flick, then turned back to meet Hernán's eyes. Hers were wet, her mouth ajar. She knew. Of course she knew.

"If he..." she whispered.

"I told you that we would find a way."

She steeled herself with a deep breath, then said, "You can't do this every week."

It took a moment for Hernán to find the words. "I'll figure out next week when it's here."

Hernán kept their guests' glasses full. Jhon said they should be going soon, his speech slurring a bit. Flick argued, took a swig, and asked for more. Hernán indulged him and let the Americano entertain them with stories from the Estados

Unidos. Flick appeared to enjoy being the foreigner in the room. He told stories about the seawalls and streets of New Miami. Whether they were true wasn't important. All that seemed to matter to Flick was that he had another refill. And another.

When Mateo went to his room for the night, Frances found a set of cards and suggested they play a few rounds. Her hands shook when she tried to shuffle them. She blamed it on low blood sugar, and handed the deck to Hernán. As they played, Flick appeared to be swimming in his own head, struggling to remember the rules of the game. He and Jhon played on a team, though Jhon did most of the work. Jhon laughed it off and said he was used to that.

During their second game, Flick leaned back in his chair, exuding confidence in his hand as he accidentally revealed a row of face cards to everyone. Jhon buried his face in his hands. Flick lost his balance and toppled backward onto the floor.

That put an end to the evening. Flick and Jhon's apartment, thankfully, was just one floor above. Hernán helped carry Flick up the stairs and put him into bed. Flick muttered something about friends and ninjas most of the way there. It was mostly incomprehensible.

Hernán found a bucket in the closet and put it by the bedside in case they'd need it during the night. Jhon thanked him profusely, sweat on his brow. Hernán insisted it was the least he could do and left their apartment, feeling like he might need a bucket for himself.

When he returned, Frances was quiet. Moments ago, the apartment had been alive, but then... Hernán started to put away the playing cards, but stopped halfway through and went to bed. He couldn't look at them anymore. He had work in the morning.

Flick, unfortunately, would be too hung over.

Hernán licked his chapped lips and tasted blood. The seasons were changing, and the air was getting dry. He retrieved the lip balm from his pocket and applied a thick coat.

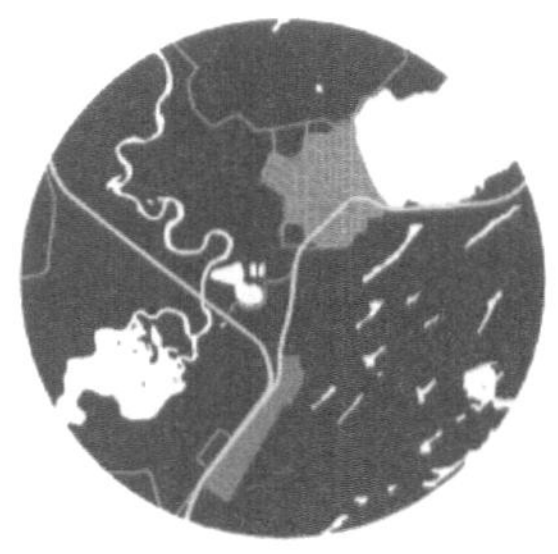

36 Broadway Avenue

Wawa, Ontario — 2128

THE THING PEOPLE FORGOT about mods was—in most cases—they only enhanced what a person could already do. Heatsinks helped miners withstand crushing temperatures as they burrowed into the Earth. Shock absorbers helped soldiers travel longer distances. Biocompressors could help the brain process information faster, if installed correctly. Of course, that was the case for any mod. Neural mods were hard to get, but if somebody could, they *got* them. Lately, a person needed something to set themselves apart. Outside the arts and Olympics, skill alone didn't get anyone far. That was what Alis' dad always said, at least.

Alis was having biocompressors installed the next day. She wondered, imagining the scalpel that would cut into her in less than twenty-four hours, if she should have gotten into painting instead. She had plenty of cozmod installations—a little body sculpting around her stomach and face, pink glow wire to illuminate her left arm and hand, with tinted eyes to match. However, none of those procedures had required anyone to dig through grey matter. Alis knew that she could call it off last minute. Her parents would be upset—Dad would be upset—but they'd get over it.

Her current situation convinced Alis otherwise.

Alis sat in the co-pilot's seat of a small, single-engine plane. In the pilot's seat, Uncle Briggs gripped the control stick. He tapped it with one of his metal fingers, keeping time with some beat that played only in his head. When he adjusted his control stick, another one in front of Alis moved in tandem.

She kept her hands in her pockets. Whenever Alis had her hands free, she tended to grab the stick. It wasn't something she thought about, it just *happened*. Last time, Briggs said that he wouldn't take her flying anymore if she did it again. Alis wasn't sure how serious his threat was, but she erred on the side of caution: hands in pockets throughout the entire flight.

Uncle Briggs banked right, tracing a path over Lake Superior's coastline. They passed over the Pic River, skirting past the Pukaskwa National Park. Alis knew that part of the country well. She'd spent most of her time near there, at home in the small town of Wawa. It was little more than a way station for people traveling along the Trans-Canada Highway, except during tourist season. Alis had swum the lakes, walked the trails, hiked up half the mountains, and skied down the rest. This was her backyard. However, from the sky, during autumn, everything looked completely different. Myriad lakes dotted the land, their surfaces shining like shards of a broken mirror. Lake Superior stretched out like a sparkling blanket, so vast that it touched the horizon at its furthest point. The forest was so dense it was a muddy brown except where the sunlight touched, which made it shine in hues of gold, crimson, and orange. Even the pines became a vibrant, minty green.

This was why Alis was getting biocompressors. She would have been more anxious about the installation if she were getting it alone. Thankfully, that wasn't the case. Léa was getting hers at the same time. Her best friend insisted on doing it with her after she found out Alis was having them installed. If something went wrong, at least they would go through it together.

"Alis," Uncle Briggs said, his voice coming through Alis' headset, "you want to take control for a sec?"

Alis blinked. "Yes," she said. Her heart raced, and her mouth dried. She was suddenly aware of her hands and how sweaty they felt. Had they been like that the whole time? She wiped them off on her jeans, but they still felt damp. She wiped harder.

Briggs laughed. "Relax. You're not landing, or anything. Just keep us level and follow the coastline. You know how to steer?"

"Rudder pedals."

"Just the pedals closest to you. And gentle movements only. And be careful with the stick. You shouldn't need to pitch or roll the boat at all."

She nodded.

"Do I need to hardwire?"

"No," Briggs said. He gestured at the wire coming from a mod in his wrist, plugged into the plane's console. "This old thing doesn't give me any info you can't already see on the screens in front of you. Tub's too old for a direct connection to mean much. Can't even get a proper connection to the Net from here, but that's part of why I like it."

"Right, okay."

"Good. You ready?"

No. "Yes," Alis said.

"Grab hold of the stick."

Alis gripped the control stick. As she did, the wiring under her left arm illuminated the cabin in a soft pink glow. Uncle Briggs grunted at it but said nothing. The plane's two control sticks moved in tandem. She could feel Briggs' grip on his through the one in her hands—his slight adjustments and imprecise motor functions. The trim was correcting his flight path, keeping the craft stabilized. As he banked slightly to the left, she felt the control stick in her hand shift with his. It was like he was handing off a baton. Every movement amplified.

Then, nothing. No sense that he was there at all. It was just Alis and the plane. The engine shook the craft, sending vibrations through her hands and arms and resonating in her chest. Its dull roar seeped through the cups of her headset.

"You let go," she said.

"I did," Briggs said. His words came like a laugh. "What did you think I was going to do?"

Alis shrugged, and the plane began to roll left. She shouted and pulled the control stick to the right, but the landscape below didn't look right. Alis checked the compass and realized that she'd put them on a path south, soaring toward Michigan.

"Level out and bank left," Briggs said. "Gently. You just over-corrected yourself, not a big deal. Good. You're doing fine. Just breathe, relax."

"Don't tell me to relax."

Alis kept the control stick steady and pressed the left rudder pedal. The world shifted underneath her again, and she slowly returned to the Pukaskwa's golden-green forests. She checked the flight display. Alis wasn't entirely sure what everything on it meant, but she recognized a few of the gauges from flight simulators and videos of pilots flying. The plane was level, and it was at about the same altitude as before Briggs handed her control. Most of that was probably thanks to the plane correcting her mistakes, but it did that for her uncle, as well.

"I figured it'd be good to see what this feels like before the doc messes with your head tomorrow," Briggs said. "Is this everything you hoped it would be?"

"I'm *flying*," she whispered.

Her uncle laughed. "Yeah, you are."

The plane bobbed, as if she'd hit a speed bump. She instinctively gripped the control stick tighter, but wasn't sure what to do next.

Uncle Briggs took his control stick back into his hands. She felt him grab it through hers—like they were holding hands through the engine again.

"Let go," he said.

She did as she was instructed and the plane leveled out.

"Just a little turbulence. It happens, especially at this altitude. Don't worry about it. You did well."

Alis glanced away from him, smiling as she returned her hands back to her pockets.

"Thanks," she said.

True freedom was rare and fleeting, but Alis felt it for a few beautiful minutes when she flew Uncle Briggs' plane. She wanted nothing more than to get back in the sky and feel that moment of weightlessness: as they left the Earth and gravity was replaced by the engine's rumble in her bones.

Alis watched videos of pilots flying, giving tours of their planes, anything she could find. They were still playing on her tablet when she finally passed out. When she woke, it was alongside the sunrise. Alis went out to the porch in a light jacket, watching the sky change from orange to peach to blue. She only left when she began to lose feeling in her fingertips.

Inside, Alis followed the sound of eggs sizzling. Her mother was in the kitchen, dark circles under her eyes. She'd probably also gotten up early. Mom never slept well when Dad was away. Unfortunately, that happened quite often lately. Work kept him busy as his company won more contracts down in the States. Mr. Walsh was everybody's friend down there.

"I started making you breakfast," Mom said, "but then I remembered you're fasting for the installation."

"Unfortunately. It wouldn't be so bad if I could at least drink something. Then I could at least make a smoothie."

"I don't think it works that way." After a brief pause, she added, "Big day."

"Mm-hmm." Alis took a seat at the table. She could have killed for some of those eggs. Would the surgeons know if she had a small bite, just to stave off the hunger a bit? "Can't say I'm thrilled to have some doc decorate my brain like a Christmas tree, through."

"I don't blame you, but your father's already sniffed out the clinic, and they seem great. Niel, one of your father's friends—do you remember him? Blonde guy from the police who was at our Christmas party last year. Kind of short. It doesn't matter. The point is that he used them to install some high-end chrome just a few months ago, and he's doing great. It'll be good for you. Biocompressors will help you stand out when you apply for the flight academy, and should the worst happen, you'll be better equipped to keep yourself from crashing."

"You think about me crashing planes *way* too often."

"I think they'll be useful for you in a lot of ways, actually. If your father's any indication, they'll help you in ways you don't even understand yet. And, yes, I'm most thankful they'll help you avoid crashing planes. I just don't like the idea of you flying around the skies in a tin can."

"Uncle Briggs does, and you don't complain about it."

"Briggs isn't the best model for what is safe and what is not."

"What's that supposed to mean?"

Mom shrugged. "He got mixed up with a bad crowd when he was your age, chasing thrills."

"I'm sure it wasn't anything too bad."

"No? Well, first it was betting on street races, then he started participating in them. Sneaking out after midnight, stealing Dad's car, hot-wiring it once when he couldn't get the keys."

"No way. Was he any good?"

"Good enough to compete with the best from here to Toronto. But he wasn't *the* best. You could only do that once you started lying and cheating, and my brother always had a strong moral compass. He wasn't meant for that world, no matter how much he wanted to be a part of it." She paused for a moment. Then, "Briggs nearly died one night. He was speeding through Tollendal at two in the morning and got pushed off the road. The car took a dive into the lake. Nowhere too deep, thankfully, but he didn't come out unscathed. The airbags broke a few of his fingers and one or two ribs."

Mom turned off the stovetop and took the eggs off the burner, plating them. Alis thought back to Briggs' metal fingers, tapping on the control stick. She'd never given them much thought before.

"Wow. Did he keep racing after that accident?" Alis asked.

"No. Officially, your grandfather put an end to it. He was furious at Briggs for a while after the accident. Once we knew he was going to recover, at least. But even if Dad hadn't put his foot down, Briggs was always more subdued after that night. He still loves driving—and flying, I suppose—but not like he used to. God, Alis, there was this look in his eye. Back then..."

"He's after the freedom the races gave him," Alis said, "not just going fast."

"Yeah. I guess you would know, huh?"

Alis shrugged. "I guess."

Léa arrived with her father shortly after eight o'clock, dressed in a cute black top and jacket with dark red pants. She was decked out in chrome, with red glow wiring wrapped around her arms, neck, and back. She'd replaced a few fingers with metal ones after a skiing accident a few years ago and recently installed a state-of-the-art hard wire in her wrist and a black box on the side of her head that served as an external memory. Her hair was dyed red as well, braided and streaked with blue. She was stunning.

All Alis could say was, "Your hair."

"What, is it okay?" Léa asked. She tucked a loose strand behind her ear, but some of it got caught in the seams around her external memory.

"Yeah."

"Chat in the car, girls," Mom said, walking past them toward the vehicle. "Hey, Mr. Oulette. Glad you could join us. Alis, hurry up. Lots of road to cover this morning!"

They got on the highway, passing Wawa's famous Canada goose statue as they headed south. They were headed toward The Neon Dragon, in the Canadian half of Sault Ste. Marie. It was one of the closest places that would install neural mods. She'd never visited, but it was good enough for Dad, it was good enough for Alis. She just wished he could have been with them.

The drive was about two and a half hours through hilly forests and around innumerable small lakes. When the wind picked up, falling leaves struck their windshield before sliding off the car. They listened to music most of the way: a playlist of Mom Pop with some singles that Alis had introduced her to, most of it dreadfully old. Léa's father sometimes spoke up, commenting on how he hadn't heard an artist or song since he was in university, and each time Alis or Léa would catch the other's eye, smirking.

They parked on Queen Street beside a brick building that was probably a century old. The place could have been mistaken for an antique store if one ignored the titular dragon hanging in the window with *Mods* written below it. Beside it, a few Japanese characters glowed neon red. At least, she thought they were Japanese. Perhaps that was something she could learn after the surgery. She'd always liked the look of Japanese calligraphy.

"Ready?" Léa asked.

"I think so," Alis said.

Mom put a hand on Alis' shoulder and squeezed lightly. Then, they all went inside together.

The Neon Dragon was dimly lit. An incense burner filled the room with a sweet, earthy fragrance. Sumi-e ink paintings hung around the waiting room, though they looked slightly *off*. Instead of the tall islands and winding trees the ink paintings usually depicted, they were of long coastlines and pine forests.

Mom announced they were there for the biocompressor installation. A man behind the counter handed Alis and Léa small tablets with consent forms to sign. Alis skimmed through the document. It was long, warning of a litany of side effects possible with a procedure like the one they were about to receive: itchy skin, rashes, headaches, exhaustion, scarring, and damage caused by glitching or shorting mods. It described the chance of the body rejecting the mod with an added assurance that The Neon Dragon Clinic did not install mods containing toxic materials. The document also warned about addictive habit formation, modular depersonalization disorder, dissociative identity disorder, amnesia and memory loss. At the bottom, in bold, it recommended against diving into the Net for the next six months, or installing any additional neural mods. Alis skipped to the end and found where she was supposed to sign her name. She drew her signature with a finger, then handed the form to her mother, tapping at a spot for parent or guardian permission.

"You're up," she said.

Mom skimmed the form quickly, then signed and handed it back to the man behind the counter. Léa and her dad did the same. Then, they both pressed their fingertips to a small chip reader to pay for the installations.

The surgeons came out to speak with them a few minutes later. They were heavily modded with chrome optics, synthetic wraps around their hands, and compartments in their wrists that Alis suspected contained their surgical and engineering tools. Each wore simple red scrubs. Alis almost missed the faint bloodstains on their sides. Probably just from an earlier surgery, she reassured herself.

They explained what would happen next: the installation would take up to four hours under anesthesia, and the recovery period would last up to six months. When Léa said she was supposed to start applying for university soon, one of the doctors assured her it rarely took that long, but that they should still take it slow for a few months. It would take time for their bodies and minds to acclimate to the mod. Mom was quick to voice agreement, recalling how Dad had taken five months to get back on his feet after his neural installation. Alis was sure it wouldn't take her that long. The tech was better and less invasive than when he got his mods installed. She kept that to herself, though.

The surgeons stepped away for a minute to make sure the surgical rooms were ready. Alis only had a few moments to grip Léa's hands and wish her luck.

Léa said, "I can't believe we're doing this, Ally."

"I know. In a few months, you'll be studying in Toronto, researching maps of the ocean."

"Hoping to make a few myself. Maybe I'll discover some lost pirate treasure while I'm at it."

Alis laughed. "Sounds like fun."

"And you'll be flying off..." Léa gave Alis a little shove. "You'll go wherever you want, I guess."

"Haven't decided what to do with it yet," she admitted. "I just want to be up in the clouds, up with the geese. Wherever that takes me. Your thing is so much cooler."

"Nah. You're following your dreams. That's the coolest."

Alis looked away to hide her smile.

They changed into surgical gowns and were taken into neighboring rooms with bright white lights and sanitation paper spread out over the operating table. Beside it, an assortment of tools—needles, knives, medi-gels, and stitching—were neatly arranged on a rolling table. Nearby was a case full of wires and nodes, presumably the mod that was about to be installed in Alis' head. She laid down on the operating table. It was cold and hard on her back. She wished they'd offered surgical *coats* too, or at least heated the damn thing.

The surgeon stood beside her, his eyes glowing bright red as they filled with medical data and whatever else he needed for the surgery. A few assistants joined him, faces and hair covered. The surgeon jacked into a nearby monitor and it flickered to life. One of the assistants lowered a mask over Alis' nose and mouth. She told Alis to relax and breathe in deep. It smelled like a marker.

Alis' head throbbed. Every movement sent a shock of pain down her spine. She tried to push off her blankets, but they clung to her like velcro. Somebody was talking to her, their voice worried and words muddled—as if they were speaking underwater. When Alis opened her eyes, the walls glowed white. People moved around her and spoke slowly. It felt as though the whole world had been set to 0.75x speed. A man's face appeared, his eyes like kaleidoscopes shifting and spinning in front of her. The sight of them made her dizzy. Alis shut her eyes, and darkness swallowed her.

Léa took two months to get back on her feet and immediately began applying to universities across Canada, plus a few in the United States for good measure. The University of Toronto was what she dreamed of, but if that didn't work out, her father had encouraged her to have back-ups ready. She never talked about those other schools much when she came over to visit Alis.

While Léa was sending off applications, Alis struggled to even get out of bed. She slept most of the time, dreading the lost days, but unable to do anything about it. She knew her recovery wouldn't be instant, but had suspected the clinic said six months just to cover their asses in case anything strange happened. Either something strange *had* happened, or she'd severely underestimated their honesty. She desperately hoped it was the latter.

Dad stuck close to home during those winter months. He reminded her often that she needed time to heal. "It's good that you're taking things slow," he said, as if she had a choice. He came to visit a few times each day, usually to refill her water or deliver dinner. He always stayed a few minutes afterwards to impart some advice to her, whether she asked for it or not. "Neural mods are terribly invasive. Our bodies, try as we might, haven't really changed much since we climbed out of the muck, and they're programmed to reject foreign objects. Your body is learning to accept the biocompressors, and your mind is learning to work with them. That takes time."

Alis whispered, "Léa..."

"Léa's recovery will be studied by surgeons and psychologists for ages." Alis' eyes were shut, but she could almost hear Dad's smile. "It makes absolutely no sense to me."

Alis fought to convey the storm of anxieties in her head. All that she could manage was, "The academy..."

"I've already put your application in. They want to talk with you when you've recovered."

Alis smiled. "The airfield's in Toronto."

There was a brief pause. Then she heard Mom say, "It is, sweetie."

In addition to everything else, Alis missed ski season that winter. She wasn't quite so exhausted during January, but Mom still refused to drive her to the slopes. Alis tried to argue, but too often her body betrayed her. She still slept most of the day and grew tired just from walking around the house. Alis was convinced that, if she'd just gotten a little help, she could have handled some of the easier trails just fine.

By mid-February, tourists flooded Wawa's streets, gathering for the ninth annual Winter's End Festival. The shops on Broadway Avenue were stocking up, preparing free samples, and putting out the last of their winter gear with bright yellow sale stickers on their tags. Dad was busy all week, helping them prepare for the weekend. His company was sponsoring the event again that year, and he liked to approach that with a personal touch.

"Money doesn't solve problems," he once told Alis. The memory was crystal-clear, as though it had happened the day before, even though he'd said it when she was just eight years old—speaking to her as if she weren't a child. Alis always thought Dad was a bit distant, but looking back now, she thought he just didn't know how to talk to children. She didn't know why she hadn't realized it sooner.

It was winter then. They had just moved to Wawa, and Dad was on the porch in a bright red coat, looking out over the town. Alis had just learned about homeless people. Not that she hadn't seen them in the streets before, the concept just hadn't fully *clicked* in her head until then. Once it did, Alis didn't think it was right that some people didn't have a place to sleep at night, especially when her father worked for an architectural firm. Looking back on the re-discovered memory, she could practically see the worry lines in Dad's face. He'd been just as uncomfortable as she'd been confused.

"What solves problems, then?" Alis had asked. At the time, money seemed like it could do anything. It came out of the chips installed into Mom and Dad's fingers and provided any-thing they could want. Didn't everyone have those chips?

"*People* solve problems," Dad said. "You can throw money at anything, but without good people to put it to use, you've done nothing."

Alis hadn't understood at the time. Looking back, she thought she knew what Dad had been trying to say—albeit in a very confusing way for an eight-year-old. And she wasn't sure that his argument was as air-tight as he thought. Or perhaps he knew it was flawed, and chose not to dwell on it.

Alis stood on the same porch, looking at the chip on her pointer finger. She'd gotten the wallet installed on her fifteenth birthday. Before that, she'd had to carry things around physically. It had only been a couple of years since then, but the strip of metal felt as familiar as the surrounding skin. Like it was always meant to be there.

She wondered what other memories she could access now that her biocompressors had fully assimilated. What other strangely adult conversations she'd had with her father, or crafts she'd built with her mother. They were hard to recall on her own since she wasn't sure exactly what she wanted to remember. Perhaps there were ways to help herself along, like how that spot and the chip reminded her of the talk with Dad.

Alis pulled up a guide on meditation through her lens and saved the file for later. Perhaps that would trigger something. She wondered if the incense on the video's thumbnail was required or if she could make due with one of Mom's scented candles. Alis pulled up another article about different kinds of incense and started to skim through it.

Léa sent a message. The text appeared over a long paragraph comparing the benefits of sandalwood and lavender: *[08:57] Are you going to the Winter's End Festival tomorrow?*

Alis collapsed the article and replied, *[08:58] Probably in the morning, before too many tourists show.*

[08:58] Meet you at the intersection?

[08:59] Sure. I'll be there around 9:30.

[08:59] Sg. How have you been feeling lately? Still no side effects?

[09:01] It feels strange, more focused, if that makes sense?

[09:02] I know what you mean. Things are sharper. *That's all, though? No glitches?*

[09:11] No. Not that I've noticed. Why? Have you had any?

[12:47] No.

It took Alis an hour to decide what to wear. She settled on a simple white tee with blue jeans. It was all going to be covered up by her coat, anyway. It had layered fabric, black on the outside and white on the inside, with sleeves of faux leather. She put it on, the leather cool to the touch, the wool soft and warm. As Alis stepped outside, she pulled a toque over her head, pressing her hair flat.

Snow fell gently from a sky the color of static, dusting Wawa in a thin blanket of white, brightening the surrounding mountains and hills. The police blocked off Broadway Avenue for the festival. Large orange barricades were strewn across all the intersections, leaving plenty of room for pedestrians to walk. The tourists were, unfortunately, already arriving. They strode shoulder-to-shoulder down Broadway, passing outdoor booths and metal sculptures of Canada geese, and a busker was playing a pan flute. His fingertips, red from the chill air, danced across the instrument as his music accompanied conversations and snow crunching underfoot.

Léa was already at the intersection of Broadway and Main. She had dyed her hair again, black with streaks of platinum blond, though the ends around her neck caught the light from her glow wire and shone teal. Alis texted Léa, and they met in front of the pharmacy.

"It's been so long," Alis said.

"I came to visit you all the time," Léa stated. Thin, barely visible clouds formed in her breath. Something about the way she said that made her sound like she was bored. It was probably nothing.

Alis was probably just overthinking it. "I know, but it's not like we could go anywhere or hang out much. I'd just pass out on you."

"You passed out while I was visiting *several* times."

"I'm sorry, but I've been better lately. Why haven't you come by in the past few weeks?"

"You had me thinking that I'm bad company. Didn't want to bore you too much."

"Never, I just—"

"I know, I know, I was there too. Remember? I've just been busy sending out applications. Dealing with some stuff. Almost finished with that now."

"Yeah, how come you recovered so quickly?"

Léa shrugged. "I guess I just lucked out."

"Or I was unlucky. By the way, what was that thing with you yesterday about glitches? You kind of ghosted me on that. Everything okay?"

Léa shrugged, glancing over her shoulder. "Nah, it's nothing. I was just concerned there was more to your recovery than just the *recovery*, you know? No ghost, I just didn't have more to say. And Dad's had it in for me lately. Had to step away to deal with that."

"Deal with what?"

"He says my neurals are changing me. I say he's just pissy that his daughter has her sights set on somewhere out of town. It's finally hitting him that I'm going south. Not my fault there's nothing happening in Wawa." She glanced around at the street. It was getting busier already, conversations in English and French bubbling up around them, their accents ranging from local to Québécois, to a few flavors of US American. "Well, nothing for *me* here."

"Well, the academy has my application," Alis said.

"You got in?"

"Not yet. I still need to meet with them, but Dad seems to think it won't be hard. He thinks I'm overqualified, I'm pretty sure. Anyway, I'm hoping to schedule that soon. Would love to go down and see the airfield too, but I guess that depends on how soon it is. Feeling better, but not sure I'm ready for a long trip away from home. What about you? Any news about uni?"

Léa shook her head. "I should hear back soon. Once I figure out where I'm going, I'll start getting ready for that. Already began studying some resources available online at a few of the schools to kill time since I couldn't hit the slopes."

"Next year we will," Alis said. She gave Léa a little shove. "I hope you get into Toronto. The academy isn't too far from the university. We'll be able to meet up after we're both done with classes and..."

Alis trailed off. She noticed that Léa was staring at her shoulder, where Alis had pushed her. Her gaze moved down her arm to her hands, wrapped in red glow wire. She stared at them, fingers twitching as if they were brand new.

"Are you okay?" Alis asked.

"Yeah. Fine."

Alis lowered her voice. "Hey, you can talk to me, y'know. What's going on?"

Léa sucked on her lips. When she spoke, it came as a whisper. "Be honest with me, Ally. Since the biocompressor installation, have you noticed anything strange? I talked to Dad about it, and now he thinks I'm going insane. He's got a damned psych on the line back home, trying to get me an appointment with them."

"Slow down. I don't think you're *insane*. Not any more than usual, at least. Just start over. I don't know what any of this means."

Léa took a breath. "Okay. It's like, sometimes, my body isn't really here. I feel separated from it, almost like Léa is an idea and the person who looks like her is an actor in a play I'm watching. It's not always like that. Usually things are normal, but I don't think it's right to happen at all. I read that sometimes you can ground yourself in reality by removing yourself from it, then going back. Like a reset button. So," she tapped her wrist, "I hard-wired myself to the Net and dove in, took a jog, and came back. If anything, it's gotten worse."

"Wait, you took a dive at home? Just like that? People train their whole lives to dive. They have those creepy diving rooms, or whatever they're called, just to get in an out safely."

"This chrome in our heads is premium, Ally. I retain *everything*, and I'm rediscovering memories I didn't know I'd lost. Je me souviens comment parler Français. Wǒ xuéle Zhōngwén. Once you get a bit more familiar with your biocomps, you'll find everything comes easier. Your dad's right. You're under-selling yourself at that flight academy. You should come with me to uni and get into engineering or something, I don't know. Planes need engineers, right?"

Alis blinked at her, having a little trouble processing the glitches, the fact Léa could dive, and that apparently she had become trilingual.

"Yeah," Alis said numbly, "but I want to *fly*."

"Sure, do what you want. I'm just saying. Give it some thought. We could be roomies." A flash of a smile crossed Léa's lips. It was gone as quickly as it came. "You ready to go?"

"I guess."

Léa turned on a heel and walked up Broadway Avenue. Alis followed, her mind racing. Her friend could dive now. That alone was stunning. It was also a tragedy in the making. If the wrong people found out, she'd become a target. And if the less-wrong people found out, she'd get conscripted into the special forces; not that Alis had any evidence of the government doing anything like that, it just *seemed* like a possibility. And if Canada didn't, somebody else would. Lately, everyone was snatching up people who could navigate digital space, turning them into machines of war. They were human siege weapons and defense grids, decked out with more chrome than skin.

Somehow, that was related to Léa's out-of-body experiences. That bothered Alis the most. She'd explained it already, but Alis couldn't imagine half of what Léa had said. She still had so many questions. What triggered it? What did it feel like? When did it start happening? Would the same thing happen to Alis now that she was mostly recovered? She wanted to ask, but Léa was rushing and didn't seem keen to discuss any of it right there in the middle of the festival. That was fair. Alis wouldn't have wanted to discuss glitches with her mods in such a crowded place either. Although the last glitch she had was when her glow wire wouldn't turn on.

Léa kept her hands in her pockets, head down. Alis stayed close to her. They strode past the florist, the bookshop, and the ski shop. When the crowd thinned and she could see the end of Broadway Avenue, Alis finally took Léa's hand and forced her to stop. She spun around, glancing at her hand curiously. Her gaze traced Alis' arm until their eyes met. Léa's pupils were bright red. She was searching for something on her lenses.

"Why did you stop me?" Léa asked.

"You're walking so fast. The festival's back there. We're practically at the end of the street."

"We're practically at PasNet."

Alis glanced over Léa's shoulder. At the intersection ahead of them stood the PasNet office, a recent addition to the neighborhood, built to provide better internet connections to people between the major centers in Toronto and Winnipeg. Alis had never so much as glanced inside its tinted windows. She'd just been glad to see the abandoned *36 on Broadway* diner replaced by something that didn't look destitute.

"There's a whole market back there," Alis said, "and you want to visit the *data center*?"

Léa shook her hand free of Alis'. "I have to. Listen, I'm glad you're not experiencing whatever I am—at least not yet—but something's wrong with me. Just *walking* here feels wrong. I haven't been able to figure out why, but with a hard link to PasNet's systems, maybe I could find something. And if you start having the same issues, I can fix them for you too."

Alis felt a chill run down her spine.

"I'm sorry I didn't say anything about it sooner," Léa said, "but we need to keep moving."

"You never wanted to go to the festival."

Léa pursed her lips. "No, I didn't."

"So, why invite me?"

"I thought you might want answers, too. I assumed you were experiencing the same things I was. Maybe I assumed wrong. I'm glad. That gives me some information though—something about your biocomps are different from mine. Was it the surgeon? Or maybe your longer recovery time prevented whatever this is. What blood type are you?"

"What? I don't know. Who just knows that?"

"I'm B positive." Léa shrugged.

"And I love that for you."

"Hm. Listen, I don't *need* your help, but I would much prefer to have it. When I dive, I'm totally unaware of my body. It's... It's freeing, but it poses a real risk. Not like I expect any trouble in Wawa of all places, but it would make me feel better if you stood watch for me."

"What if I tell you no? Look, this is weird, Léa. You're acting... You're not yourself."

"God, you sound like my dad. Look, it doesn't matter. I'm trying to find out why this is happening, but to do that I need to tap into PasNet's link. I need a better connection than I can get at home. If you don't want to help, you can go, but I'm doing this."

Alis gripped her toque. It nearly fell off her head, and she pulled it tighter. Snow clung to her fingers. This was insane. Léa was insane. "*Fine.* Tell me what to do."

Léa gave her a quick nod. "Let's go."

Alis took stock of the intersection she'd been led to: the garage, the data center, the shops, and the apartments stacked above them. The police station was just up the road. Alis didn't see their cars around, though. Maybe the officers were all down on the lower half of Broadway where it was busier.

Léa spoke while she walked toward the data center. "I don't know how long I'll be out. I haven't tried something this complicated before. Shouldn't be more than a half hour, I think."

"That long?"

"Probably less. Aiming for fifteen minutes, but time is weird on the other side. Things don't match up quite right, or at least they don't *seem* to. I'm still getting the hang of it."

"Don't you think you shouldn't be diving if you're still getting the hang of it?"

"You're right. But my..."

Léa trailed off. Her gaze shifted down to her feet on the crosswalk. She stood still, feet firmly in the slush. Around her, the slow morning traffic ground to a halt. Somebody honked their horn. Alis took Léa's hand and pulled her toward the sidewalk. She moved stiffly, as if each step was a burden.

Then, her body loosened up, and Léa continued, "...symptoms are becoming more pronounced. At this—"

"What the hell was that?" Alis interrupted her.

"What do you mean?"

"What do you mean, 'what do you mean?' You just froze up in the middle of the fucking road."

Léa frowned. "Interesting. Let me check my exmem."

Alis waited as Léa tapped the thin box on the side of her head and brought up a video on her external memory. She could almost see it—walking down Broadway from Léa's perspective—through the lenses on her eyes.

"Interesting," Léa repeated, her lenses flickering. "That's the first time I've been unaware of a... I've been calling them *glitches*. I don't know if that's right."

"What exactly is going on?"

"I told you. Sometimes it's like I'm not here in my body, like I'm just observing it. And now, I suppose I'm losing the ability to tell when it's happening. I think that's worse."

"It definitely *sounds* worse. And you think hacking into PasNet's systems will fix it?"

"No, but I may be able to get some answers. Lots of research and studies are being done on neurals that are still hush-hush. Documents tied to military-grade stuff."

"Wait, you're going to use PasNet to look at restricted files?"

"If I need to. Don't look so shocked, Ally. Half the Net is built on one military's hardware or another's, all stitched together with a little copper wire. If that fails, I may be able to access my biocomps' files from the other side. They started as MG tech before going into the public, so they must have something I can use. Not sure if that will work, but I need to try. Come on." Léa renewed her stride toward PasNet, glancing up at something—one of the building's many security cameras. Alis hadn't even considered them. She was about to say something when she noticed Léa's eyes were bright red. As the light faded, she said, "PasNet won't see us. I've blinded their cams."

"That was easy."

Léa grinned wickedly. "I found a good hook-up while you were napping. Neon Dragon quality, but with none of the forms or questions they shoved in our faces. The lady even gave me a discount."

"Not sure I wanted to know all that."

"It's fine. Everyone's got a back-alley mod or two, right?"

"Did you get any others I should be aware of?"

Léa grinned at her, then picked up her speed. Alis followed her to an alley between PasNet and *Café Rush*, a coffee shop. It was a narrow, unpaved path covered in a dusting of snow. They found an access point on the wall outside of the data center, a metal box that was connected to some thick wiring, near where the alley met with the sidewalk. Alis moved a few trash bins while Léa opened the box, revealing a collection of switches, wires, and ports. Léa pulled a wire from her wrist and jacked into one of the ports.

"So, I just stand here while you...?" Alis asked, uncertain what to expect. She'd only seen a dive in the movies.

"Don't let us get seen. If you do, and somebody comes asking questions, get them to leave and make sure they don't try to alert PasNet. Or call the police. Don't let anyone jack me out mid-dive, either, whatever you do. Shouldn't have to worry about any of that, though. Ideally, I'm out for a minute, and when I'm back, I'll have an idea what's going on. How to fix myself. We'll both be safe, and I can finally focus on uni again."

"And we can go walk around Broadway after?"

Léa smiled, and her glow flickered off. "Yeah, sure. I'd like that."

Alis opened her mouth to say something else but thought better of it.

"What?" Léa asked.

"Just... Don't get lost in there."

"I wouldn't dare," Léa said. She winked at Alis with red eyes, flicked a switch, and collapsed in the snow.

Alis took a few deep breaths and extinguished the pink glow wire around her arm. Everything about this was *wrong*, but if it helped fix Léa, then it was worth it. Right? Alis steadied her nerves and helped Léa sit against the wall, making sure to tuck her legs behind the trash bins so that nobody walking to the festival would notice her. When that was done, she squeezed herself next to Léa, trying to make herself as small as possible to avoid being seen. She had no idea what she would do if anyone saw them.

They sat in the alleyway like that for some time. Alis occupied herself by reading the meditation articles she'd saved earlier, watching the snow fall, and brushing it off Léa when a dusting began to pile up on her head and shoulders. Léa's legs kept stretching out, and each time, Alis' heart jumped. She pulled them in close and held them in place, making sure they were out of sight.

After nearly half an hour, Alis' butt was freezing cold, having nowhere to sit but in the snow and mud. Her coat was soiled around the bottom hemming and her pants were probably ruined. Alis wondered what she should do if Léa was still mid-dive after another half hour or longer. At what point should she *actually* start worrying? Alis looked up some articles on her lens. A few suggested calling for help after twenty minutes, others said after sixty. It was impossible to tell which was right.

Worse, somebody would notice, eventually. That, she was relatively certain of. Whether it was PasNet, the police, or somebody on the street walking just a bit too close to the alley, they couldn't hide there forever. Jacking Léa out was also not an option, though. Disrupting a diver's connection could cause lasting damage. That was how all the divers in movies got caught. Sometimes they lost all sense of reality afterward. Sometimes they died from the shock of coming back into the Real.

Alis heard the coffee shop's door slam shut. Footsteps approached, crunching snow. Alis made herself small, curling up, and made sure to keep Léa's body from unraveling. So far, that had been enough to keep them hidden.

The footsteps stopped right next to them. Alis glanced up. The bin's lid lifted, obscuring whoever stood on the other side. She heard a heavy bag fall to the bottom, and the lid swung back down. In its place, Alis saw a woman. Her hair, just beginning to show signs of grey, spilled out from under her cap and over her shoulders. She had left behind her coat, despite it being cold enough for her breath to come out in white clouds. A brown *Café Rush* pin was fixed onto her breast pocket.

"What..." the woman started, eyes following the wire connecting Léa and the PasNet building.

"Please," Alis said, "my friend's sick. She's trying to figure out what's wrong, and she said this would be the best place for her to find answers. I know it looks bad, but that's it. We're not stealing anything. I'm just watching over her while she looks for answers."

"Okay," the woman said. She didn't seem particularly convinced.

"I need to know that you won't call anyone."

The woman nodded slowly.

"She'll be done soon, and we'll be on our way. I promise. You'll see."

The woman hesitated a moment, then hurried back into the coffee shop.

When Alis heard the door slam shut, she took Léa's head into her hands. Her eyes were moving beneath closed lids, like she was dreaming. Alis pried one open, hoping she could wake her up without pulling the plug. Of course, it did nothing. She let Léa close her eyes and whispered, "I don't think you have much longer in there. I don't know if you can hear me, Léa, but you need to get out. Now."

Léa sat still in the snow and mud, her mouth slightly ajar and her body limp.

"I mean it, Léa. I don't care if you got what you came for or not. You can try again later, but right now, I need you back."

Léa's breathing was steady, her chest rising and falling slowly, breath misting in the air.

"I need you back," Alis whispered. A chill touched her spine.

Alis tried jacking Léa into a port on her own arm, hoping that she might be able to talk with Léa that way, but nothing happened. She unplugged and the wire snapped back into Léa's arm. Alis slapped Léa's face, pretty certain that wasn't the right way to wake her up either. She tried running a quick search on her lens for what to do, but the query only turned up recent news articles and videos of glitching mods and psychotic chromeheads lashing out. Then, sirens filled Broadway Avenue. Cars rumbled to a stop in front of the coffee shop, casting red and blue light across the walls.

Doors slammed shut.

Alis swallowed hard.

"Hey there," a man's voice said, made mechanical by an amplifier mod. "My name's Niel. We got word that a girl might be diving 'round here."

Alis scanned the box Léa was plugged into, searching for a way to remove her from it. Red text and diagrams flashed in front of her eyes: information about broadcasting systems, network infrastructure, and a thousand other things all at once. She didn't see anything about how to wake Léa. She changed some of the search parameters and tried again. Footsteps approached, sliding on slush, then crunching on a thin layer of snow.

"We're just trying to understand what's going on, and make sure everybody's safe," Niel said through the amplifier. He spoke a little louder now. "Is there somebody we can talk with?"

Alis checked again to see if there was a way out. Police cars had appeared on the other end of the alley as well, and she still hadn't found a way to safely unplug Léa. Her search was still running, but with each article, news story, opinion piece, and user post, she became increasingly worried that she wouldn't find anything. She took a deep breath and stood.

Only one police car had come to the front of the coffee shop. One officer, who had been approaching the alley, stopped when Alis saw her. Her hair was wavy, and she wore a navy blue uniform with the letters *WPD* stitched onto her jacket's sleeve. A man, probably Niel, stood beside the car. He was short, a little heavyset, with a beard that obscured a mod implanted around his neck—the amplifier. He looked familiar.

The man's eyes showed a flash of red. What was that? Was he talking to his partner, or running a facial recognition scan on her, or something else?

"Hi there. I'm Niel," he repeated in a half-mechanical voice, "and this is my partner, Inez."

"Hey," Inez said, as if she hadn't just been sneaking up on Alis.

"And just so you know," Niel said, "a friend of ours is behind you on the other end of the alley. He's not trying to surprise you, just trying to make sure everyone is safe."

"We're not trying to hurt anyone," Alis said.

"Alright. Do you mind if—I'm sorry, are you Kevin Walsh's daughter?"

Alis frowned. "Yeah," she said.

"Well shoot," Niel said, in his natural voice, without the amplifier. "I worked with your father on a few projects before I joined the force."

"You were at the Christmas party."

"Last year, yeah. I was sorry to miss you lot at the Hendersons' this year." Niel laughed. "Kevin's girl. Let me tell you, Wawa is a small place. You see a lot of familiar faces responding to calls, but I can't say I expected to see you. Do you mind if my partner and I take a few steps closer, so we can talk easier?"

Alis looked around. The scene was drawing attention. Other officers appeared from around the corner and began to corral a gathering crowd back toward the shops. Some people went about their business. Others just found a new vantage point from which to watch.

"Yeah, that's fine," she said.

Niel and Inez approached with slow, measured steps. Niel looked confident, no, comfortable. He'd done this before. He was probably good at negotiating with people, figuring out and diffusing situations. That meant that his partner was the hammer. When things went wrong, she was probably the one to bail them out of trouble. They both carried pistols, but Inez held a hand close to hers, ready to draw on Alis if she needed to. She wouldn't need to. Alis was certain of that. But she wasn't certain that she could convince a trigger-happy cop of the same.

"Wait," Alis said, and pointed at Inez. "You stay."

"Alright," Niel said, and a flash of red appeared briefly across his eyes. "Can I ask why?"

"She's too ready to draw her weapon."

"Inez won't draw on you. But, if you insist."

"You don't even know if she's armed," Inez hissed at him.

"I'm not," Alis said quickly, and raised her hands so they could see she wasn't holding anything.

Another flash of red over Niel's lens—then the same over his partner's. They were sending messages to each other. Whatever he'd told her, it must have been convincing. Inez took a step back and put her hands on her hips.

"Keep your hands on that bin," Inez said as the red faded from her eyes. "Don't take them off."

"Okay," Alis said, and put her hands on the trash bin, fingers splayed through the dusting of snow that had gathered there. She glanced back at Léa, wondering how she would get them both out of this without a criminal record. Perhaps that window had already shut.

Niel's smile faded as he got close enough to see Léa. "Why don't you tell us about what's going on. Is she a friend of yours?"

"Yeah," Alis said. Perhaps it was best to just tell them the truth. That way, they couldn't charge her for lying to the police. She wasn't sure if that sort of thing held any weight in court, but it *felt* like it might.

"Mm-hmm," Niel said. No notes, no questions. Even the red over his eyes had faded away. He was just focused on her and Léa.

"She's sick," Alis said. "I think. It's hard to understand, but we both got some new mods installed a few months ago. She's been having some side effects. She described it like an out-of-body experience. And she froze up on the way here and acted like she didn't even notice it happened."

"It sounds scary," Niel said.

"It was. It is. She was *convinced* she could find answers if she jacked directly into PasNet's systems. I don't know why she thinks that will work, but she does. That's all she's doing. Looking for answers. She's trying to fix herself."

Herself and me, Alis thought, remembering Léa's concerns that Alis would have the same glitches soon. That didn't seem like something she needed to share, though.

"That's one way to go about it. There are doctors and clinics who specialize in helping people navigate new mods, as well as any side effects they might offer. Has she tried any of them?"

"I don't know. I haven't spoken to her much lately."

"Hm. Inez is a pretty experienced diver. If you let her jack in too, she can reach out to your friend and bring her back. It'll just take a few minutes, then we can get out of the cold. We'll grab a couple of coffees down at the station while we sort all this out. What do you say?"

Alis balled her hands into fists, keeping them on the trash bin, the metal and snow turning her fingers a shade of pink.

"I don't trust her."

Inez rolled her eyes. It happened so quickly that Alis almost missed it.

"Do you trust me?" Niel asked.

Alis shrugged. "Maybe a little."

"Okay." He laughed. "We're getting somewhere. You don't have to trust her, just trust me. I've known Inez for the better part of a decade. She's always had my back, and *I* think letting her jack in is the best thing we can do right now. You're a smart kid, Alis. You know that the longer we wait the more your friend is in danger."

"How long's your friend been under?" Inez asked.

"I don't know exactly. Maybe forty minutes."

"That's a good trip. She's been diving long?"

"Only for a month, maybe less."

"Shit," Inez said. Alis even caught Niel's placid expression break for a moment.

"Is that bad? What's it mean?"

"Diving's an unnatural thing," Niel explained. "It messes with your body. It *really* messes with your mind. People normally have to work up to half-hour trips. Inez can go a bit longer without issue since she's been diving for years. Somebody as fresh as your friend should have ejected after a few minutes. She—"

Inez interrupted him, "Your friend's at risk of losing her mind."

"No," Alis whispered.

"We need to act quickly," Niel said. Red flashed across his eyes, then vanished just as quickly. "Will you let Inez jack in so she can try to save her?"

Alis hesitated—then chastised herself for hesitating. If what they said was even half true, there was no time to waste.

"Okay," Alis said, then moved aside to let the officers in.

Inez acted quickly. She rolled up a sleeve exposing a dense layer of chrome wrapped around her wrist and arm. She pulled a hardwire from it—one of many—and jacked into one of the ports beside Léa. As she did, her eyes lit up red.

"What's her name?" Inez asked.

"Léa."

"Got it. Just to be clear, I don't know if this will work, but it's our best shot at getting her out safely. Either way, it shouldn't take more than a couple minutes. Then we'll know more."

Inez sat down next to Léa and closed her eyes. A moment later, her body slumped against PasNet's wall.

"She's done this before?" Alis asked.

"Yeah," Niel said. "Kids like your friend think they can take on the world. It's part of being young. It's just that in the past, that used to manifest in simpler ways. They'd dive off bridges or drive fast. The Net's become a similar problem lately. I've never heard of somebody who's lasted this long with this little experience, though. If that girl makes it out okay, I could see her having a bright future in Net Ops."

Alis frowned. "She'd turn it down."

"Yeah? What's she want to do?"

"She's going to university this year to study geographic science and climatology."

Niel raised his eyebrows.

"Léa's so excited about it."

"Good for her. Inez is going to do her best. I also called a few other officers to help us. Paramedics will be with them to help your friend if she needs it when she comes out of her dive."

"And if Léa doesn't come out with your partner?"

"We go to plan B and pray for the best."

Niel's backup arrived a few minutes later. Police and paramedics swarmed the alley, each outfitted with bulletproof vests. The police carried riot shields and handguns. Niel assured her they were using non-lethal rounds, but it all seemed excessive.

Meanwhile, the paramedics prepared to treat Léa. They unfolded a stretcher in case she had to be carried to the ambulance and prepped some kind of headband for her. One paramedic with more chrome than skin stepped forward. He jacked into one of Inez's spare ports. He never dropped into a full dive, but his eyes lit up like a Christmas tree.

Alis and Niel stepped back a few paces to allow them more room to work. The police established a perimeter around the PasNet building using their cars and barricades as its border. The crowd was forced farther away from the alley, though many still tried their best to see what was happening. A van with *Wawa 24* plastered on the sides pulled up across the street and began filming the scene while a drone buzzed overhead.

She could just barely hear the reporter: "Thanks, Malcolm. I'm here on Broadway Avenue as the Wawa Police Department are securing a scene involving—"

Alis wanted to make them leave. She wanted to curl up and hide. She felt on-edge and numb all at once, and she didn't know what to do about any of it. A sudden breeze made Alis shiver, aggravating the way her snow- and mud-soaked pants chilled her to the bone. Niel got her a blanket from one of the paramedics, which helped, but what she needed was a change of clothes.

"How much longer do you think this will take?" she asked.

Niel shrugged. "Your guess is as good as mine. I would have expected something should have happened by now, though."

"Do you think something's wrong?"

"The Net is a strange place. I've never been there, but Inez tells me things about it. How things are real and not real all at once. Roads, bodies, information—it all exists in multiple states at once. You have to piece it all together just to navigate, and not everyone pieces those things together the same way. At least, that's what she told me."

"What does any of that mean?"

"I haven't got a clue."

After a long silence, Niel stepped forward and asked the other officers how things were going. Alis followed closely. The paramedic with all the chrome pivoted to look at him, his eyes a storm of red and blue. She couldn't tell if any part of them was organic anymore.

"I'm giving Sergeant Vachon another couple of minutes, then I'm going to bring her back."

"You can bring people back?" Alis asked? "Just like that?"

The man scowled at her. "I can act as their *sherpa*. I guide people home, but you can't guide the unwilling. The Sergeant is attempting to do the same for the girl, but trying to force it tends to just entrench them deeper into the Net."

Niel asked, "Has Inez found her yet?"

"Traces of her, like fragments. She says…" The chrome man's jaw slacked a bit, his eyes wandering, then he snapped back to. "She found the girl."

Alis gripped the blanket tighter.

"Excellent," Niel said. "Bring them back. She's been in for way too long."

"I can't," the paramedic said. His voice curdled like sour milk. "Girl's refusing to come out."

"Tell her I'm here," Alis said. "Tell her Alis wants her to come back."

The chrome man gazed off into the distance. "Girl told the Sergeant that she's not finished. Whatever that means."

A chill traveled up Alis' spine.

The paramedic's eyes flashed and he retracted the wire that connected him to Inez's wrist. A few seconds later Inez snapped back into reality. She rolled over and coughed like she'd been drowning. Spit and bile dripped off her lips, melting the snow. She glanced up at Niel and grumbled, "That girl's short-circuited."

"What happened?" Niel asked.

"I don't know. It's like she's part of the Net. I can find her, and I can't. I can reach out to her, but when I do, she's wiped a whole cluster. Never seen anything like it." Inez's gaze shifted toward Alis. With a sneer, she said, "Your friend's diving like she's been doing it all her life. I can't keep up."

"Maybe you're not as good as you thought," Alis said. She regretted the words as soon as she saw Inez's glare. "I mean—"

"*Nobody* of sound mind could keep up with that girl." Inez's boots scraped against the cold, muddy ground as she stood up, holding herself against the wall for support. One of the paramedics tried to help her up, but she shooed them away. "Listen, I know you're struggling here, but Léa is lost. She's been diving too long. Should have come out a long time ago."

A moment of silence passed. The breeze caught Alis again, despite her blanket. It seemed nothing could ward off the cold.

"What now?" Alis asked.

"Plan B," Niel said, his eyes a bright red.

Before Alis could react, the police readied their riot shields, drew their weapons, and the chrome man ripped Léa's hard-wire out of the box. Her body wretched upward, screaming, gasping, and clawing at her wrist as the cable retracted back into it. The glow wire around her arms shorted, flashing red before going dark. The chrome man's eyes flashed, and she spun on him, pulling the pistol from his holster and shooting him in the stomach with it. He dropped hard, metallic hands dripping in blood. The police stepped between him and Léa. Somebody shouted at her to surrender. Léa fired the pistol again and again at the officers in front of her. Those behind her seized up as if possessed, while others stumbled as she shut off their optic mods. Alis' ears rang and her head throbbed. It only took Léa a few seconds to nearly dismantle the officers surrounding her. Those remaining upright were barely able to maintain the shield wall they'd encircled her with.

Alis moved without thinking. She shoved past Niel, but somebody grabbed her wrist. Inez. Alis twisted her arm and pulled harder and screamed, but Niel had taken her other hand, and they held Alis back together. They were shouting something, but Alis didn't catch it.

"Léa!" Alis shouted to her from behind the wall of riot shields.

Léa stared back, lenses flashing red, her body breaking into spasms. She was panting, teeth bared, with the pistol still firmly in her hands. Her hair clung to her face, soaked from snowmelt. Alis could hear shouting in the distance. Cars honking. The sun reflected off the riot shields and blurred her vision.

"You said you wouldn't get lost," Alis said. Tears streamed down her cheeks.

Léa flung herself forward, screaming like a banshee. Shots fired, closer this time.

Léa collapsed in the muddy alley, centimeters from Alis.

After the incident, Léa was taken to Toronto General Hospital. She was given a windowless room with a door that locked from the outside. Her room was part of what was unofficially called the Glitch Ward, where engineers worked alongside the hospital's doctors and surgeons. It was the first of only a few facilities like it in the country. The entire floor was full of broken things: the victims of bad chrome, most bolted behind heavy doors. The ward looked like a prison, but once she got over that, the place gave Alis hope that somebody would be able to wake Léa from her coma. Alis participated in tests as well, visiting a few times to check her vitals and scan the biocompressors in her head. Meanwhile, the police investigated The Neon Dragon clinic, reviewing their tech and interviewing the surgeons. They hadn't found anything yet.

By summer's end, with the air conditioning whirring above her and Léa withering away in a white hospital gown, Alis came to accept the truth. Nobody in the Glitch Ward had any idea what they were doing, and none of the tests they ran on her would help Léa. They were just keeping people comfortable and studying them so that they might help the *next* patient.

Alis ran her hands through her hair. She used to talk to Léa when she came to visit, but it was hard to see the point in that now. Even if some part of Léa heard what she said, did it matter? The person that had lashed out that morning on Broadway Avenue wasn't *her*. It was in her body, but Léa wouldn't have done any of that. She couldn't have. All that Léa ever wanted to do was help people.

Guilt weighed on Alis like an avalanche. Léa hadn't planned on installing any neurals until Alis mentioned she was getting biocompressors ahead of applying for the academy. That knowledge alone made it nearly impossible to get out of bed. She never said the words aloud because she knew nobody would understand, but Alis should have been the one to glitch. It was all her idea from the start. Léa still had so much to live for.

Alis excused herself from the room. She told her mother and Uncle Briggs, who'd come with her on the final day of testing, that she needed to go get some air. She took the elevator down to the ground floor, which was packed with the ill and injured, all waiting for a room to open up. There were never enough.

Dozens watched Alis leave the building, no doubt hoping her departure meant that one of them would win the lottery and be seen soon. She couldn't meet their eyes.

The hospital had outgrown its place in downtown Toronto. It was a mass of concrete, steel, and glass that spread out in all directions, some of it suspended over the surrounding roads. Skyways connected the main hospital to in-network and partner facilities like the lab and children's hospital. In narrow gaps between those buildings and the sidewalks, somebody had found room to grow grass and rows of dense green bushes. There were flower boxes affixed to the first-floor windows filled with geraniums and a leafy plant that Alis' lens told her was a *premium sun coleus*.

She found a bench in the shade near the hospital's entrance. She could already feel sweat forming down her back. Léa would have hated how humid it was.

After a while, Mom and Briggs found her.

"Hey," Mom said. "We were just headed over to the café across the street. Your uncle can't deal with the hospital's coffee."

"I don't know why anyone would when there's a café literally right next door," he said.

"Right," Mom said. "You want to come with us?"

Alis nodded.

Mom got an iced coffee for herself and Uncle Briggs each. Alis picked out a bottle of cherry pop, Léa's favorite. They sat in the café, taking a table just beside the AC. Not directly under the vents, but close enough that Alis got goosebumps along her arm.

After Briggs had drunk half of his coffee, he said, "I heard the academy approved you for their next cohort. You excited to finally start?"

It should have been an easy question. Instead, Alis felt her gut twisting under the pressure. "About that," she said. Mom's eyebrow arched in a way befitting a cartoon character. "Don't be mad, but I don't think I want to go to the academy anymore."

Mom sighed. "This is all you've talked about for *years*, Alis."

"I know, I'm sorry."

Briggs sipped his coffee, ice rattling in the cup.

After a moment, Mom leaned forward and asked, "What is it you want to do?"

"I've been thinking about this a lot since, you know. Especially after seeing how the ward works, how nobody there really seems to get treated. They just manage the problem or get studied like a lab rat. I don't want what happened to Léa to happen to anyone else, and if there's even a chance we can bring her back, I have to take it. So, I've been looking around at programs in body modifications. Specifically, the engineering and medical programs."

Mom exhaled. "That's a big change."

"Yeah."

"And you thought I'd be mad?"

"I don't know. It's just so last-minute. I'm not even sure if I can get into university this year. And the academy has already—"

"The University of Toronto's just down the road," Briggs said, gesturing to the street.

"Why don't we check it out?" Mom asked. "If we go now, we might be able to talk with somebody before the office closes."

"Really?" Alis asked.

"Yeah. Grab your drink. Let's get out of here."

"Okay. What do you think Dad will say when he finds out?"

"He'll be *thrilled*," Briggs said, laughing. "Your old man was always going to support you, but you're lying to yourself if you thought he was excited about you flying."

"Briggs," Mom hissed at him.

Alis laughed. "No, he's right. But... I'll bet *you* could still teach me to fly, Uncle Briggs. Maybe when I'm on holiday, if you're around, you can show me how to run your prop. Not just steer, but everything else too."

Uncle Briggs grinned. "I'd like that."

The Beast of Longyearbyen

Longyearbyen, Norway — 2130

THE ATLANTIC SHONE UNDER the summer sun, though the view was obscured by dark rain clouds that lay between it and Kanan's flight. The scene turned his stomach. There was far too much water. All he could imagine was his plane malfunctioning, plunging into the depths, salty water suffocating his bones.

Kanan shut his window blind and took a slow, deliberate breath, returning his attention to his tablet. He reminded himself that he'd been through far worse than a transatlantic flight. He had spent the last two years in California, where he reported on the war for the *Digital Inquirer*. He'd witnessed countless attacks through the Net and saw special forces steal—or attempt to steal—artificial intelligences. Several of his friends had been caught in the crossfire: researchers and engineers at Cephas Neu, Traveler Technologies, and other government-funded labs. Kanan himself had only narrowly avoided death or overloading on no less than three separate occasions.

He still didn't know exactly what the warring parties were after or what the consequences would be, even with his media clearance. Although, perhaps the corps were keeping him in the dark *because* of his media clearance. That seemed more likely.

An uneasy peace had fallen over the Pacific in the past year, and it seemed to be sticking, at least for the time being. As glad as Kanan was for that, headlines about peace didn't sell subscriptions. So, the *Inquirer* gave him a new assignment and put him on a plane bound for Longyearbyen, Svalbard.

A century prior, Svalbard was a barren archipelago best known for its snowmobile tours and nature reserves. That changed drastically as the arctic warmed. The islands stood high enough to avoid the worst of the rising oceans, and although the new climate had damaged the local ecosystem, it made life easier for people to live there. The state of Norway recognized the archipelago's potential in the 2060s and marketed Svalbard as a slice of the old world—"a glimpse of life as it used to be." They even constructed a stage in Longyearbyen as the town grew into a city, where Norway hosted Eurovision in both 2072 and 2120. Afterward, much of that construction was replaced with local housing and businesses. No amount of urban sprawl could satisfy the demand for either. Even the once-abandoned town of Pyramiden had sprung new life, as a few Russian mega-corps sought to profit off the area's population boom.

Kanan was looking forward to his time on Svalbard. His supervisor had said the assignment would be like a vacation, but he was determined to stay on task. Despite the relaxed briefing, something odd was happening in Longyearbyen, and it all centered around Norske Oseaniske Løsninger. The Norwegian-based company, best known for its fish farms which fed millions, was breaking into other forms of mariculture: farming shellfish, seaweed, and algae.

The company's CEO was away from the archipelago that week attending meetings in Oslo. The *Inquirer* hoped that with her away, Kanan might get some answers from her staff about their missing funding. He had already lined up a meeting with one man—Agnar Andreassen. A technician at the company. Likely too low-level to have knowledge of what might be going with their finances, but he could have heard people talk. After all, for as much as Longyearbyen had grown, it was still a small city compared to the likes of New York or Tokyo, constrained by the surrounding mountains. If nothing else, Agnar might be able to provide the names of people who knew more.

Kanan spent his time on the flight reviewing Agnar's file, digging into NOL's business, and researching Svalbard at large. The evidence was thin—even Kanan had to admit that—but some of the numbers weren't adding up. The United States and Western European Union had invested in NOL's mariculture projects, but it didn't seem like all that money was actually going toward those projects. Normally, that sort of thing wouldn't have been worth his time, but as land-based food became increasingly more difficult to farm, mariculture was becoming a topic of much attention. People were invested in mariculture's success, so it stood to reason that they'd be interested in a headline about NOL's finances.

It was probably a simple case. Criminals weren't nearly as clever as films and books made them out to be. The simpler a plot, the more easily it could be overlooked and the more successful they usually were. The situation was probably caused by some low-level staffer skimming money off the top. Somebody who had access, was careful about never taking too much, and only skimmed from deals made behind closed doors, out of the public's eye.

Or perhaps there was some kind of embarrassing secret. The CEO's son had recently begun working at the company. She could be protecting him from some mistake he made, siphoning money to pay off a debt he owed. It wasn't a difficult thing to imagine—even if the boy's record was clean. Every mega-corp heir could afford a clean record.

Whatever the case, if the perpetrator was caught, it would be big news, and it would be a divisive story. Ignoring the legal ramifications, stealing from a mega-corp was the sort of thing the people rallied behind lately. Kanan had seen it play out just a few months prior: after authorities detained a man for theft from a few of the Detroit-based mega-corps, the locals started calling him *Robin Hood*. He was gone—his body missing (probably at the bottom of Lake Erie)—but people still talked about Robin of Detroit.

Regardless, Kanan hoped it was just a simple fraud case. For once, he didn't want a complicated problem to solve. A simple investigation, with some time to enjoy the city of Longyear-byen, sounded like exactly what he needed.

Kanan's plane landed at Svalbard Airport at 22:00 local time, and the sun was still in the sky. He had slept during the flight, but not enough. A shot of espresso from the airport café helped pick him up.

He collected his luggage and boarded a small white bus. Kanan found a seat by a window and retrieved a pack of ciga-rettes from his bag. He lit it and brought it to his lips, breathing deeply. Immediately, he felt his muscles relax, and he breathed a trail of smoke out through the open window.

Kanan had studied the maps, but being in Longyearbyen felt different. The city reached around Adventfjorden, swallowing the ancient settlements there. Hiorthhamn, Advent City, Nybyen, and even the old satellite station had been incorporated as neighborhoods. Around it, the mountains stood tall. Some bore roads carved into their façades, leading up into small suburbs through pine forests.

Downtown Longyearbyen, where the old town once stood, was like any other city. The streets buzzed with the movement of taxis and buses—there were shockingly few personal vehicles. Advertisements clung to and exceeded the height of skyscrapers, flashing images of attractive people promoting a drink or film. Many bore some form of the Norwegian flag, whether it was part of their outfit, on the product, or elsewhere. The space between was filled with smoke, shadows, and a neon haze that clung to the air like water on a dog. To Kanan, it felt rather quaint.

Kanan found his hotel on Vei 36. His room was small, no more than a hundred square feet. It was barely enough space for a bed and restroom, with a small folding desk built into one of the walls. It wasn't much, but it was all he needed for the week.

He pried open the blackout shutters and peered through the window. The golden glow of the sun illuminated the city below. He checked the time on his lens: 22:46. The sun would not set until summer was over. What an odd thing to behold, to be normal.

Kanan closed the shutters and went downstairs into a ramen place that he'd spied on the way to the hotel. He found a seat at the bar and ordered a spicy hasselnøtt Tantanmen with pork ribs. It was prepared like Kanan remembered from his time in Japan, just made with slightly different ingredients. The hazelnut sauce had a lovely, subtle spice, and the noodles had a stronger wheat taste—though not so much that it distracted from the rest of the meal.

"It's all local ingredients," one of the staff said after Kanan asked about the dish. "Well, local to the mainland. Most of it's from Norway and Sweden. Some of the sauces, we can only get from Japan."

"I imagine you can't grow much on these islands, with all the mountains," Kanan said.

"Tsk. A few try, but there's no space for a farm. Nothing on the scale the city needs. Ocean's a different story, though. Plenty of that to go around."

Agnar Andreassen was a mid-level technician overseeing NOL's offshore farms. The file that Kanan had on the man was thin. He opened it again the next morning and re-read its contents: two pages detailing Agnar's work history and one containing a few details on his personal life. Agnar had a history in tech, a relationship with an Englishman who moved there a few years prior, and a pair of cats at home. Kanan checked the man's social feeds to see if he could find anything there, but most of it was just pictures and videos of the cats lazing in the sun or sticking their tongues out. It was little leverage, but better to know who he was meeting than the alternative.

The city was quieter that morning, but the distant sound of water and sails and shouting suggested the action had simply moved toward the bay. Kanan hailed a taxi which took him as far as the Adventelva River bridge, where traffic slowed to a crawl. Kanan walked the rest of the way to Old Advent. The whole neighborhood smelled of fish and soil. Agnar was at a bar across from the NOL offices there. It was a bit close for Kanan's comfort—he wasn't ready for anyone at the company to know that he was digging into their business—but it wasn't even 10:00 yet. Most people would be busy working.

The bar, *The Old Anchor*, was lit in neon purple and green with a nautical motif beneath it. Only one man sat at the bar. He was slightly overweight, his clothes were a size too small, and his hair was shaved along the sides. Chrome wrapped around his head, and his right hand had been replaced with a metal one, his fingers an intricate array of extendable points and joints. A wire threaded from the gauntlet up his arm, under his sleeve, and reemerged attached to a port on the back of his neck.

"Sorry I'm a few minutes late," Kanan said as he took a seat beside him. "Interesting choice of meeting place."

"Nobody drinks this morning," Agnar said in broken English. "You have the translate?"

"I do."

"[Good, because this conversation would have taken twice as long if I had to try and speak in your confusing tongue the whole time.]"

Captions appeared across Kanan's vision a moment after Agnar spoke in Norwegian. Kanan could pick out a few of the words before translation appeared, but not enough to keep pace.

"We good to talk here?"

"[The door was unlocked only because I requested it. It's not open for business until noon, and the owner is a personal friend. She is in the kitchen, preparing for this evening,]" he said, then switched to English: "We will not be bothered."

"Good. This should be quick anyway. The mariculture project NOL is working on, tell me what you know about it."

"[I spend most of my days repairing the farms. I could tell you about how they work, or where they are, if that helps.]"

"What do you know about the project's donors? Or any recent projects they've been funding?"

"[You are aware you're speaking with a mechanic, right?]" Agnar asked. To emphasize his point, his eyes flashed yellow, and he gestured with his mechanical arm. His fingers made a clicking sound as he tapped them together. "[Whatever questions you have about the donors, I don't have a hand in that.]"

"I understand, but you're on the ground. Have you seen anything that might be sapping money away from the mariculture projects? It could be somebody on your staff who is suddenly wearing designer clothes, or the company taking on extra projects..."

"[Nothing like what you describe.]"

"Alright, let's try this another way," Kanan said. He took a breath. "Tell me about your typical day at NOL. Don't skip a beat, no matter how boring or mundane a task it is."

Agnar thought for a moment before answering.

"[I begin at 8:00. It is easy this time of year, since the sun is always up... This is what you want?]"

"Keep going."

"[If you wish. After arriving, I review paperwork. These are reports about what has broken overnight, or what is *still* broken. My priority each day is to make those repairs. That may take all day, depending on what happened. Lately, it takes all day.]"

"Why do you have so many repairs?"

"[Because of the attacks.]"

"Attacks?"

"[Have you not heard of the monster?]"

"No."

He grinned. "[There is a beast in the depths. Few have seen it. Fewer live to tell their tale. It comes when the sun is lowest in the sky and attacks the farms. It breaks them apart, feeding on the herring and salmon and whatever else is in them. It tends to avoid the new algae farms though.]"

"That's impossible. Something must have been stolen aside from the fish. Or maybe it's a rival sabotaging the project while they build their own farms. Wouldn't be the first time a corp pulled a stunt like this, and I know of at least half a dozen other corps making a move on mariculture who would love access to NOL's systems—or to see them disrupted."

"[It is no pirate, no sabotage. I told you, it is a beast.]"

Kanan resisted the urge to roll his eyes. Instead, he asked, "How often are you attacked?"

"[Lately, it has been at least once a week.]"

"What's NOL doing about it?"

He shrugged. "[Not much to do while the beast lives.]"

"So they're not doing anything?"

"[They're trying to establish protection, and are moving some farms closer to land, where they can. I believe they're preparing to build a better fence. I will probably be building that this autumn.]"

"Can they move the fish into the bay?"

"[No. There are more farms than you realize. They surround half the island, they would never fit in such a small space. And even for those that *are* near Adventfjorden, there is a great deal of red tape. Ships need to come and go too. More likely, the company would pick somewhere less populated. Better for people too. Nobody likes the smell of fish all day and night. It's extra-strong where NOL shows up. Some of the people have begun to complain about what we have now.]"

Kanan ran a search through his lens. Most of the news covering the beast's attacks were in the tabloids. The local news had covered some sailing accidents but didn't spend much time discussing the alleged sea monster. A broader search through Norway's mainland network was of little help.

Kanan closed the search when he began to see articles about the Loch Ness Monster. "You mentioned that some of the people who saw the *beast* are still alive."

"[A few.]"

"Where can I find them?"

Agnar gave him a list of names and locations—though most were only vague approximations. He knew some of the survivor's usual spots, but little beyond that. It was enough to get Kanan started, though. Once he met them face-to-face, he would be able to tell if Agnar's story was a farce or if there really was something to the beast of Longyearbyen.

Kanan wired Agnar his fee. A feed on his lens showed the withdrawal, and a moment later, Agnar's lens glowed a bright yellow in response.

Everyone back in New York was going to love this story. Kanan the monster-hunter. He could imagine their cheshire grins. Perhaps he'd slay the beast and bring its head back to the *Inquirer*. They could mount it on the wall for all to see and inscribe into the plaque: "'Twas brillig, the slithy toves."

He stifled a laugh.

If anything, Kanan was convinced that this was the work of some pirates in a submersible; a rival trying to cut NOL's projects off at the knees, or thieves using the *beast* as a cover. He'd seen as much during the war. No matter the outcome of a raid, both sides would deny it ever happened because they couldn't afford to let the public become aware of what was protected or stolen. If a few documents went missing and the herring's pen was broken, the latter was sure to be the object of people's attention. NOL would make sure of that. Though, Kanan had to admit that it was odd that the pirates weren't targeting any of the new algae farms.

Agnar laughed, breaking Kanan out of his thoughts.

"What's so funny?"

"[Nothing.]"

"Is it about NOL?"

Agnar sighed. "[It is about you, American. You flew all the way here, called upon me—paid me—for information you could have gotten from anyone here. It is as if I flew to meet you in Upper New York to ask you where to get pizza by the slice. Far too much effort for far too little reward. All for a story not worth following at that. And unlike my curiosity in New York pizza, this journey will just get you killed.]" Agnar stood. "[But I do appreciate your business. I'm planning on proposing soon. My boyfriend's ring just got a bit shinier. Thanks for that.]"

Before Agnar left, Kanan called over his shoulder, "Don't get the shiniest stone."

"[Why not?]" Agnar paused at the door.

"You want people to think you have been saving for that ring, not that you suddenly got the money from somewhere. Too shiny, and you may turn NOL's head as well as your man's."

Agnar grinned. "[That is smart, sir.]"

Kanan sat in the empty bar a moment longer. He didn't want to risk being seen walking out with Agnar, just in case anyone was wondering why he had gone into a closed bar so early in the morning. While he waited, Kanan did another search for anything about the beast. He found some more reports of ships being damaged, sailors lost at sea, and an interview with Elena Aaberg—one of the survivors Agnar mentioned. Perhaps that was something, but it was hard to tell. Everything he found had happened recently, within the last few weeks. When he checked Norway's mainland news outlets, nothing. Whatever Agnar knew—whatever the city knew—it had yet to leave the island. Or the technician was talking out of his ass. Kanan breathed a heavy sigh and stood up. Either way, it was his only lead.

Kanan tried a bar near the bridge first and asked a few people there about Elena. He found somebody who knew her among the staff, but she had moved back to the mainland a few weeks prior. Nobody there had her contact info. Perhaps he could dig that up later, but for the time being, Kanan moved on to the next name on Agnar's list.

At a coffee shop downtown, Kanan inquired about a German named Sören. One of the baristas called him *Sören the Black*, on account of his usual order. The man was a regular patron but hadn't been around for over a week.

Aase was supposed to be at the pier. By noon, Kanan found a sailor who knew her name, but he said she was in the hospital recovering from an attack. Last he knew, she was unconscious.

When pressed, the man said, as if it were a normal thing to say, "[She was caught in the beast's wrath.]"

Assuming Aase was still unconscious, Filippa Tennfjord was his last chance at getting an eyewitness account of whatever was happening at Longyearbyen. To find her, Kanan had to travel through Platåberget, a neighborhood elevated on a wide, flat summit of the same name. It was a newer part of the city. Its streets were lined with tall buildings that served as shops, offices, and apartments all in one. It was just as crowded as downtown, but there were more pedestrian paths. Kanan walked shoulder-to-shoulder through a marketplace, the air filled with buskers' acoustic guitars and his stomach tempted by street vendors—Norwegian waffles, sausage rolls, and freshly baked cardamom buns.

Along the southwestern edge of Platåberget lay Bjørndalen, an old coal mining town on the edge of the city. It existed within a small, flat valley at the end of a steep staircase. A road was being constructed between the two, but as yet was not completed.

Kanan spied his destination as he made the descent: a small shop with a large greenhouse attached. The sign on the front read, *The Root Vault*. Inside, the shop was painted green, and its shelves were occupied by vegetables and spices. Potatoes, turnips, beets, ginger, onions, and more filled the air with a pungent, earthy odor. Kanan picked up a ginger root and ran a thumb along the rough surface. He hadn't seen real ginger on a counter like that since his time in Japan. In the States, it was always kept behind the counter under a glass display case.

"[Good morning,]" a woman greeted him in Norwegian. He set the ginger down and turned around to face her. She had blonde hair that touched her shoulders and wore a shirt and jeans, both stained by soil and clay. She rested a calloused hand on the counter between them and her sleeve shifted, revealing a white bandage wrapped around her wrist.

"Morning," he said.

"[Ah, can you understand me?]"

"I can. Speak any language you like. I'm translating it."

"[If you like, but I do not have a way to translate you.]"

"Tell me if you need me to repeat anything, then."

She nodded.

"Your shop's name is cute," he said. "The Root Vault."

"[It is named after the seed vault in Platåberget. You've heard of it? People here are proud of the place, and this started with my mother's family growing root vegetables, so it made sense. This was her idea.]"

"Why root vegetables?"

"[They're hardier. Today, you could grow wheat or barley in a few places, but not much of it. And such crops were practically impossible back when my family started this place. Roots, on the other hand, won't get damaged in high winds.

They aren't bothered much by a frost. And, everyone loves a good potato.]"

She paused, looking Kanan over as if sizing him up.

"[You're not here about the greenhouse, though. Tourists stick to downtown and the mountain trails. A local wouldn't even remark on the name. What is your business here, sir?]"

Kanan leaned against the counter. "You're an observant one. Most people get to talking and it doesn't matter who they're talking to."

She blinked at him.

"I'm looking for Filippa Tennfjord," he said. "A friend told me she was working here now."

"[What friend?]"

"A sailor she knows. I didn't get a name. 'Friend' may have been a bit of a strong term, I'll admit." He smiled, trying to put a friendly face on over the lie.

"[Filippa is busy.]"

"So, she *is* here," Kanan said. "I just need to talk with her. It's for a piece with the *Inquirer*. You can come with me to see her, if you like. It'll just take a few minutes, then I'll be on my way. Here," Kanan said, and retrieved a business card from his back pocket. It was an archaic thing, easily damaged, but the *Inquirer* had a fondness for legacy media.

She still hesitated. The woman glanced back toward the door to the greenhouse, then up at the roof—no, at a security camera.

Kanan wired the woman a few thousand krone. A yellow light flickered over her eyes as the transaction completed. "It's important to me," he said, putting the card away.

She sighed. "[I am Filippa Tennfjord,]" she said.

"I thought you might be. The bandage gave it away. My name's Kanan Hamilton, nice to meet you. You were caught up in an accident at sea, from what I heard. One of only a few survivors of that and similar attacks."

"[I'm sorry, you speak so quickly.]"

"Apologies. The accident at sea—"

"[The beast in the ocean.]" Filippa crossed her arms and receded toward the wall behind her.

"The *beast*. What can you tell me about it?"

"[No more than I told] Norske Oseaniske Løsninger [when they came for answers, or the police after them. I don't know what you hope to uncover that they could not.]"

"NOL took a statement too?"

Filippa nodded. "[It is a bitter memory, but I've told it in hopes that it helps somebody kill the beast. I suppose you want to hear it as well.]"

"If you don't mind."

"[It happened late at night, with the sun low on the horizon. The glare off the water made it hard to see anything. We were sailing back with our catch when it struck.]" She winced, as if the memory bore teeth.

"Take your time," Kanan said.

She took a breath and leaned against the wall. "[It hit the boat and knocked Christof over the rail. We tried to get him out, but it kept hitting us from all sides, like a wrecking ball. I saw a flash of something whenever it struck the hull, but never a good look.]"

"It was definitely an animal? Not a submarine or—"

"[It was a *monster*,]" she said. "[It killed everyone else on that ship. We lost the fish we'd caught. I only survived because a NOL ship was nearby. They arrived in time for me to jump on deck as my ship sank.]"

"NOL's ship didn't get attacked?"

"[One of the sailors thought the beast was distracted by our catch. The hull was damaged, and fish spilled out into the ocean. Perhaps it was feeding. Whatever the reason, it was a small mercy.]"

Kanan frowned. The fish farms and a fishing boat; wherever the beast attacked, it did seem to be after food. That appeared to invalidate his theory about pirates and thieves. They would have been after tech, money, or people to ransom—not *fish*. However, the alternative still didn't make any sense to him.

Animals didn't just attack randomly. Perhaps the group who carried out these attacks were hungry. Revolutionary whispers had begun to creep into political discourse, but it was hard to imagine anyone was actually acting on that. Certainly not to such an extent that they might starve themselves.

"Where were you attacked?" Kanan asked.

"[Near Kongsfjorden, northwest of here, around morning. Best to avoid it though.]"

"Appreciate the concern," Kanan said. However, he still wasn't convinced that this wasn't just a red herring. Only one way to find out, though. "What about the other attacks? Any idea where those happened?"

"[I don't know. All over the islands. I'm tired of talking about this. It was an awful night—one that I hope never to relive. I'm not going sailing anymore. Took up the family business, finally.]"

He nodded, recording a note on his lens about Kongsfjorden.

"[I always thought I'd end up here again,]" Filippa continued. "[I just thought I'd get a few more years on the waves first. Oh, well.]"

"People like to make plans, but the world likes to spit in our faces."

She smiled. "[I like that. Is that a saying in the United States?]"

"Nah, it's just something my father used to say."

It took a few hours, but Kanan convinced a fisherman to take him to Kongsfjorden the following morning. He passed the hours until then in the ramen shop by his hotel, enjoying the relative quiet of the place and a fresh bowl of shoyu ramen, served with chashu pork.

After his meal, Kanan walked around downtown. He had no destination—which was an odd feeling—but he enjoyed seeing the city. Here, it was easy to forget that mountains and ocean surrounded them. The city almost looked like a modern megacity, except with some of Europe's old-world charm. After all, Longyearbyen had once been a remote town of only a few thousand. It had been the frontier upon which humanity came to research the arctic and hike the trails. To an extent, that was still the case. The seed vault and all the old laboratories were still there. The rest of the world had just moved in alongside them, seeking refuge from the heat, floods, and fires elsewhere.

The sun remained in the sky through the night again. Kanan arrived at the pier early, as an orange glow spread over the water, and the sky was shades of pink and red. He met with the captain, Víðir Ingólfsson, who carried a large rifle over his shoulder. Several among his crew carried rifles as well. A precaution, he explained, in case they really did find the beast.

Before they left, the captain offered Kanan a chance to call the voyage off. "I won't charge you for the trouble," he said with a slight accent. "My crew and I will just go out fishing like normal. If I were you—"

"I'm getting tired of everyone telling me how to do my job," Kanan said, and walked aboard Víðir's ship. There may be something in the ocean, but it certainly wasn't a sea monster, beast, or whatever the locals wanted to call it. Once he confirmed that, the veil would lift. Or, at least, he would be able to return to investigating NOL without all of these distractions.

Víðir's ship was factory new. It wasn't large, but it made good use of the space it had, with several tanks below the deck for the fish they caught and a cabin so dense with shiny instruments that it resembled a plane's cockpit. It was a wonder there were any fish left in the Atlantic with gear like this.

Kanan paid the first half of Víðir's fee for the trip. The rest would follow once they returned. With that done, the old man's crew was quick to unfurl the sails and steer out of Adventfjorden. As they turned north, Víðir found Kanan on the ship's prow. "So," he said, "how many men turned your little adventure down before you found us?"

"Thirteen before we spoke."

He laughed. "Svalbard's an old place. Lots of hardship here, lots of blood, especially for the families who lived here before it was comfortable. They're a superstitious lot, and it's rubbed off on most."

"You don't believe in the beast, then?"

"[It's not a sea monster,]" he said in Icelandic. Then, switching back to English, "Probably a corp covering up a mistake. They come from outside, like me and mine, and they can see how willing the folk are to believe such things. If they can use that to their benefit, they will. But that's not a good thing. I'd wrestle with a mysterious fish over a corp any day. You should know. You've got the [stink] of a corp about you. Or maybe it's just your *Americanisms*. You lot are always working some angle."

Kanan grinned. "I was a cog in the wheel once. I still am, but not in the same way."

"Eh, that's what they all say. Tell yourself whatever you like. Doesn't bother me, but you can't honestly tell me that one corp is better than another. They're all shit, just in different ways. We have our pick of working for the abusive shitbags, the irresponsible shitbags, or the back-stabbing shitbags."

Kanan laughed.

"Laugh if it helps you sleep at night," Víðir said. "Whatever helps you look at yourself in the mirror. But you're young. You still have time to get out."

"Which corp loans you this ship?" Kanan asked.

Víðir's mirth fell, and his face turned a shade of red.

"My guess is Vikinson. It's a Norwegian company, and they operate in these waters, don't they? Renting out ships to fishermen so they can work—but most of your catch goes back to Vikinson. At least until you can pay off the debt. But they only offer new, state-of-the-art ships. Fresh equipment. Makes your job easier, but makes going fully independent tough, doesn't it? This is a lot of ship to pay off."

Víðir leaned against the railing and sighed deeply. "They take all of it," he said. "Not most of the catch. All of it."

When they arrived in the waters where Filippa said the beast attacked her crew, Kanan began recording with his lens. A red light blinked in the corner of his vision. After that, there was little else to do but wait for something to happen.

After some time, he asked Víðir to bait the water. The crew were hesitant, but the old man convinced them to do as he said, reminding them they'd brought rifles for a reason. After they threw the fish overboard, the crew began patrolling the ship like a private militia, eyes locked on the waves below.

Kanan wasn't sure what to expect. The notion that he was hunting a sea monster was foolish. He'd been swept up in the locals' steadfast superstitions. He believed there was indeed something—more likely someone—damaging NOL's farms. Clearly, people had been hurt in the process. It was an easy leap to assume that needing to monitor and repair the damage was what sapped the company's resources. It was also convenient that there were so few survivors.

If Kanan could get the right ledgers—if such ledgers existed—he would probably find the missing money matched up with the cost of repairs and protective measures they'd taken. The secrecy was odd, but perhaps NOL was afraid of admitting the problem was something they didn't understand yet. The world would have laughed at them if they announced they were grappling with a sea monster.

Kanan had paid for Víðir's crew until noon. Probably nothing would happen, which made the venture a good chance to relax under the endless arctic sunshine. He watched the waves. The bait attracted fish. Kanan couldn't see them in the dark waters with the sun's glare striking his eyes, but he could see the spray they caused as they fought one another to feed. Víðir said they were salmon. Kanan didn't realize salmon ate meat, but he took the old man's word for it.

As the salmon's feeding slowed down and the bait diminished, another lull fell around the ship. Kanan knew they were all thinking the same thing: the trip had been a waste of time. Although, the locals on the crew were probably quite pleased about that.

They baited the water a second time, a little while after the salmon left. The fish returned quickly, creating another frenzy around the ship's hull. Again, after a few minutes, a lull fell over the ship. The sun was nearing its zenith, casting a glare across the water. The sky had turned a shade of blue, marred only by a couple of grey clouds slowly rolling in. They looked ready to burst, but Kanan couldn't tell if the storm would pass overhead or if they'd dodge it.

The captain was walking over toward Kanan again when one of his crew called his name from the cabin. He spoke with her in Icelandic, too distant for the translator to work. Kanan walked over to join them, intending to tell the captain it was time that they turned back. This whole trip was pointless, and he didn't want to be the reason they got caught in a storm. It was time that he returned to shore and worked on finding those ledgers.

"[—make sense,]" the woman finished telling Víðir as Kanan approached.

"[The stupid machine is broken again,]" Víðir said. "[I told the inspector it wasn't right, but of course they didn't do anything about it. Just checked the box on the form.]"

"[When it happened last month, a reset fixed it, though.]"

Víðir noticed Kanan and gave him a friendly smile. "Nothing to worry about," he said in English. Then, to the woman, "[It only worked after a couple resets. Did you try that?]"

"[Four times.]"

"[Four times?]"

"[Yes. If it is still broken, it's worse than before the inspector looked at it. It's not just glitching, it's giving a false reading. Or something *is* out there.]"

The boat rocked suddenly, as if they'd run aground. The jolt sent Kanan's shoulder into the wall and nearly made the captain fall over.

"[Reset the scanner again,]" Víðir told the woman. Then, shouting past Kanan, "[And somebody check whatever we just drifted into!]"

"[We haven't been drifting,]" one of the crew shouted back.

At that, several of the armed crew members took their rifles off their shoulders and inched toward the railing. Kanan followed suit and walked the edge of the ship. He leaned over the rail, peering into the water below. A few of the crew joined him, readying their rifles and shouting in a mix of Icelandic and Norwegian. The water below was dark and ever-shifting. Sunlight flickered off the waves and ripples. A shadow shifted below the surface, something larger than the salmon feeding before. Kanan leaned further forward, trying to catch a glimpse, to record it, and the boat was struck again.

Kanan felt the sea surge around him before he realized what had happened. His clothes dragged against him, and his shoes were filled with cool water. Salt filled his mouth and stung his eyes. Kanan felt weightless and heavy all at once, heart racing, the ocean suffocating him.

He forced his eyes open, determined to film whatever had struck Víðir's ship. The blinking red dot in his lens blinked back at him, flashing erratically as the water pressed against his lens.

A shadow reappeared in the water. Something was swimming ahead of him—toward him. Then there were more. Dozens of massive shapes emerging from the dark. The closest one was headed directly toward him, its face becoming clearer: black skin, white eyes and jaw, teeth bared, blindingly fast. He thought he heard it screaming, muffled by the water.

Kanan tried to swim out of the way, clawing at the ocean, but the creature rammed into him all the same. He felt his back collide with the ship's hull—then nothing. He felt nothing. Kanan couldn't move, no matter how hard he tried. He tasted salt in his mouth. He heard the muffled sounds of the ship being rammed above and bullets puncturing water. Somebody else from above fell overboard as one of the creatures rammed the hull again. He didn't glance at Kanan—just dropped his rifle and swam toward the surface.

A pressure rose in Kanan's chest as the sea threatened to fill his lungs. Slowly, the taste, the sounds, and the pressure all faded away.

Kanan closed his eyes and sank into the dark.

External Memory

Dandridge, Tennessee — 2149

MR. MILLER ARRIVED AT the hospital early that morning, just before 9:00 AM. He complained of stinging pains, nausea, and bloating. After an hour in the waiting room, the assistants—a small fleet of robots who helped ferry patients around the building—gave him some pain meds and promised he'd see a doctor soon. When that proved not enough, a nurse gave the old man something a bit stronger and a thirty-two-ounce glass of contrast dye. He drank it and lied down in the arms of a CT scanner. It was an archaic method, but a CT was inexpensive enough that nobody needed to contact insurance providers. On his Silver Premium plan, Mr. Miller wouldn't qualify for anything else, anyway.

When the scans arrived in Kristen's hands, she spent all of sixty seconds reviewing them before deciding his appendix had to go.

Mr. Miller was scheduled for surgery at 2:45 PM. Kristen had to stretch the truth about the severity of his condition in order to get a room, otherwise he would have waited until the following day. She had appendicitis when she was in high school and of all the classes, exams, dances, and track meets, *that* was what she remembered most: the blistering pain in her side as she walked into Mrs. Langford's Spanish class. She refused to make Mr. Miller wait as she had.

While the surgical aides prepared the room, Kristen reviewed some of the recordings on her external memory. Appendectomies were not difficult, but it had been a few weeks since her last one. Lectures from university and past surgeries flashed before her eyes. A montage of classrooms and surgical monitors—of frantic note-taking and methodical incisions—filled her vision.

When Mr. Miller arrived, wheeled in by an assistant, she was eager to begin.

Kristen was joined by an anesthesiologist to make sure Mr. Miller stayed asleep and an engineer in case of any complications with Mr. Miller's mods. None stood between her and his appendix, but he also had an external memory. Anything that touched a person's brain was a red flag, but shutting it down prior to the operation usually prevented any issues. Kristen never had problems with exmems. She had gotten hers installed just before med school. They were, by all accounts, one of the safest neural mods one could get.

But it never hurt to be careful. No tech was perfect. If today was the day one finally backfired on her during surgery, Armani was there to fix it. While she watched her surgical monitors and the anesthesiologist monitored the old man's vitals, Armani watched a feed relaying Mr. Miller's modular feedback—just as the three of them had done thousands of times before.

As the surgery began, an alert appeared on Kristen's lens. Orange text glowed across the corner of her vision: *Your 6:00 AM–3:00 PM shift has ended. You have been automatically signed out of Covenant-Sanders Medical Center. Have a nice day!*

Kristen blinked the message away and made the first incision. She removed the inflamed organ and handed it off to an attendant. The bot shuffled toward the lab, its heavy metallic steps filling the hall as she stitched the old man back up. It was over by 3:30 PM.

As Kristen was washing up, Armani tapped her on the shoulder and said, "Nice work in there."

"Thanks," Kristen said, then walked out the door.

The studio apartment's air conditioning switched on just as Kristen's keys hit the countertop. She made herself a cup of instant coffee and tossed in a splash of liqueur, stirring it together. A trail of steam wafted from her mug as she carried it to the little desk. It barely contained enough space for her computer, a couple of succulents, and a stack of old books. Real ones. The world had moved on to digital formats, but she learned to love reading paper books. She loved the leathery feel of their covers and the sweet, earthy odor they filled the room with—that old book smell. She would need a few more stacks before she could rival her father's library, though.

Real books weren't hard to get, but the market had changed immensely. The only hard copies that most sellers offered were collector's editions of whatever market-tested classic hadn't gotten one in a while or rushed limited editions of bestsellers, printed once the publisher realized they'd been caught up in the zeitgeist.

Either way, the books were beyond gorgeous, filled with art and commentary, but they were also terribly expensive. Most people weren't ready to dump a thousand dollars on a copy of *Fahrenheit 451*, no matter how the projection cover made the flames look like they sprouted off the book; the same story could be purchased for a fraction of the cost, stored on a shard or one's external memory, and read on any screen or lens.

Then, there were all the *other* old books: the sort that were lovely and important but lacked the same kinds of profit projections. Those had the inverse problem: they existed only as hard copies, forgotten in a million antique shops and grandparents' attics. Even if they were pulled out of storage and dusted off, they were too much of a gamble to re-format for digital. A waste of time.

That was why Kristen began Clingmans Press. Her small publishing house started as a fun side-project and quickly escalated out of control. She exclusively reformatted and republished books in the public domain as eBooks formatted for modern lenses and tablets. She sought old titles that other publishers dismissed, which would otherwise be forgotten completely as the ink faded and their spines broke.

Her current transcription was a thriller, nearly a century old. It was a stand-alone, thankfully. Series were a pain to track down. Its pages were brittle in her hands, and some of the ink had faded around the edges. It had probably been caught up in a flood at some point. Most books that were around during the late twenty-first century had some form of water damage. The floods had caught everyone off guard despite a plethora of warnings.

Kristen scanned the wrinkled pages with her lens. The words appeared a moment later on her computer, highlighted red wherever it detected a possible error. She paused a few times to correct a misspelling, and once to manually type a page that the scanner was having trouble with. To be fair, *she* was having trouble deciphering some of the bleeding type.

Kristen had completed fifty pages when she heard the door slam. Her boyfriend Tomas stood in front of it, a grin on his face and roses in his hands. They looked oversaturated, somehow redder than she remembered roses being.

"You're not ready," he said.

"You never told me you left work."

"But I did."

Blinking, Kristen minimized her lens' scanner and opened her messages. Sure enough, there were two missed texts from Tomas:

[04:26] Heading out.

[04:42] Will be there in 30, be ready!

"Shit," Kristen said. She put the book down. "I'm sorry, I didn't notice it. Or the time. I'll just be a minute."

"Reservation's for five-thirty," Tomas shouted after her as she ran to the restroom. "The Cantina Cabra's not far, but, you know."

"I'll be quick," she shouted as she found her makeup bag. All she needed was a little touch-up, nothing fancy. Something to make it look like she hadn't just crawled out of the hospital. Maybe a bit of blush. Kristen would have killed for a shower, but it was too late for that. She cursed herself for forgetting.

It was their anniversary. Their *first* goddamn anniversary. Her stomach turned, and she felt like she was going to throw up. Or, perhaps she was just hungry? It was impossible to tell. She hadn't eaten since lunch.

"Fucking idiot," she muttered at the mirror, too quietly for Tomas to hear her—she hoped. "You're going to screw this up."

She picked her outfit out of the dryer: an olive green top, jeans, and a cropped jacket. It was a bit wrinkled, but not too badly. Tomas wouldn't notice anyway. Besides, the jacket was her favorite. It was also just a little bit slutty, which she hoped would make up for forgetting dinner. If not, oh well. *She* liked the way it looked.

"Alright," she said, joining Tomas at the door. "I'm ready. Sorry about that."

Tomas gave her an easy shrug in response, but she caught his eyes wandering, taking her in. A whisper of an ache sprouted in her chest. The nausea she'd felt was quelled by his face. Not a hint of any text or images overlaid his eyes. Kristen lost count of the people she'd dated who would split focus with their lens while they talked to her, but Tomas wasn't like that. He was always there—especially so then, with the roses he carried into their apartment. They smelled odd. Normally, roses smelled of plastic and potpourri, but these reminded her of fresh fruit and mountain air.

A rumble in her stomach reminded her of dinner.

"Come on, I don't want to be late," she said while strapping on a pair of black shoes with a modest heel.

"Even if we were, there's lots of places close by," Tomas said.

"The Cantina's my favorite, though."

Tomas smiled at her. "I know. That's why I texted you to get ready."

"Right," she said. Whatever moment she'd almost been swept up in was certainly past. "Well, I'm ready now. Let's go."

"Did you see the roses, though?"

"The Cantina first."

"They're real roses."

"Wait, really?"

"Most of them."

"Tomas!" She laughed. "They smell incredible, but we don't have time for this. Put the flowers down and get your ass out that door. There are tacos waiting for us. Enchiladas. I need *cheese*, Tomas."

"Alright," he said, grinning at her.

She held the door open for him, waving a hand toward it.

He slapped her on the butt as he passed by.

"Oh, you're going to pay for that," she said.

"Oh, no," he mocked.

A squall struck Kristen and Tomas on their way home. They ran from awning to awning, laughing. The city of brick and steel, billboards and neon, was obscured by the rain. When they reached the apartment, Tomas pulled Kristen inside by her jacket, pressing his body against hers. His lips, soft and severe, found hers, then her neck. He sent shivers down her spine and threatened to buckle her knees. Hands ventured on their own, fingers finding their way beneath his jeans, her shirt, both wet and clinging to their skin. Kristen steered their embrace toward their bed, and Tomas followed, his feet heavy like wading through a river.

Kristen's lens lit up, orange in the corner of her blurry vision. *Dad*, it read, as a dial tone pinged in her ear. His picture was next to it, cropped out of an old family photo, when his hair was still brown and he wore lots of flannel. Impeccable timing, as always. She wanted to hang up on him, but he rarely called.

Kristen told Tomas to stop, her breath still mingling with his. As he reached a hand into the back of her jeans, she answered the call and said loudly, "Hi, Dad."

Tomas backed off, hands raised in silent surrender. She imagined those hands bound and tied to the bed, and bit her lower lip at him.

"Kristi," her father's voice came through her cochlear implant. It was urgent and restless. "I can't find your mother. I'm worried she's gone off to... To that bar. I can't remember the name. You know it, the one in the city—"

"Dad," Kristen interrupted him, but she couldn't find whatever words came next.

Kristen's mother was dead. Lung cancer took her a few years prior. She'd put up a hell of a fight, as she always did, but she wasn't missing. They'd scattered her ashes into Douglas Lake, about a mile down the road from Dad's townhouse. They'd visited the spot together a few months ago.

Kristen glanced at Tomas for help, but he was lying on the bed, belt between his teeth. Her face must have told him something was wrong because he let the belt fall. He sat up, mouthing, *What's the matter?*

"Don't go anywhere, Dad, I'll be there soon," Kristen said. She hung up the call.

"You're leaving?" Tomas asked.

Tears blurred her vision and threatened to loosen the lenses in her eyes. She blinked them away and took a few deep breaths. No time for that. She picked up her keys from the counter and found her shoes nearby. Not the polished ones she took to dinner, but her running shoes she'd worn for years, scarred by the miles and mended with glue and thread. Dad called them her mud shoes.

"My dad thinks Mom's alive and that she's at the bar where she used to gamble. And she stopped gambling after I was born. And she's, you know, in the lake. So… I don't know what to tell him, but whatever it is, I can't say it over the phone. I have to go see him. Figure out what's—Fuck!" A seam in her right shoe came undone. The tear echoed off the walls. Kristen took a moment to breathe. She could fix it later. Right then, she had to leave.

Tomas was watching her, concern plastered across his face.

"I'm sorry," she said, tying her shoelaces. "First I was late, then this—"

Tomas put a hand over hers, fingers reaching for the keys. "Let me drive," he said.

"I don't know how long this will take. I'll drive, and if I get tired, I'll just stay there or use autopilot."

"You're not using autopilot," he said.

He didn't need to spell out why. Recently there had been several accidents on the road involving cars on autopilot. Most of their passengers made it out without a scratch thanks to a coating of medi-gel, but a few never quite made it to the hospital. The automakers were monitoring the situation, apparently, but there hadn't been enough blood spilled to force any recalls yet.

"I'll drive both ways, I promise," Kristen conceded. "You have work in the morning."

"So do you. Besides, had things played out differently, we weren't going to fall asleep for at least another ten, twenty minutes."

"You fucking idiot." She laughed. "Thank you."

The drive was quiet. Normally, the highways around Knoxville were in a near-constant state of gridlock, but at that hour, with the moon high above them, I-40 was barren. Even the rain had stopped. Tomas' hands were on the wheel, his eyes fixed on the road. An electric hum filled the cabin.

Kristen stared out the window, watching the city fade into suburbia then sweeping fields of soybean and dairy farms. In the distance, as the city lights faded, the Smoky Mountains became clearer. Their silhouettes cut through the purple-grey sky. She squinted into the night, trying to spy Clingman's Dome among the Smokies.

Kristen asked Tomas to stay in the car, at least until she had a better sense of what was going on. If Dad had forgotten Mom's death, he might have forgotten about Tomas as well, and who knew what else. He agreed and told her to go on. She was grateful—though a part of her wished that he would have put up a fight. She didn't want to go in alone.

Dad's townhouse was in a nice little community with two dog parks and plenty of space to walk between them. Most of the people who lived there were his age, and the office was particularly attentive. It wasn't quite a retirement community, but it was the closest thing to one that the town of Dandridge had.

Kristen rang the doorbell. The tone was long and slow, muffled by the townhouse's walls. The door opened a moment later. Her father's attendant stood in front of her, a model two P-Body unit. The robot stood at least two heads taller than Kristen, with smooth plating over its chassis. In the gaps between plates, hydraulics and wires shifted with every movement. Its head contained just one large "eye" covered by what Kristen always thought looked an awful lot like a hood, if the wearer's head leaned forward an unnatural distance.

They got the bot when her mother became ill, but it was purchased in her dad's name, and he ended up keeping it after she passed. He said it was good for cleaning up, but Kristen always suspected that he just didn't want to live alone. She was glad to see it.

"Kristen Norwood-Díaz," the bot said without expression. Its eye refocused on something in the distance. "You are accompanied by Tomas Major."

"Tom's staying outside for now, P-Body."

"The car's engine is not running. The temperature is sixty-four degrees Fahrenheit and projected to drop to a low of sixty-one at 2:38 AM. However, Tomas Major's temperature and heart rate appear to be within the normal range."

"He'll be fine, P," she said, and nudged the bot aside so that she could pass.

The bot shut the door behind her and said, "Kristen Norwood-Díaz, I presume you are here answering the call your father made to you forty-one minutes ago."

"I am," she said. Kristen took her shoes off by the door.

"Robert Norwood-Díaz has been looking forward to your visit."

"He said Mom was missing. You know anything about that?"

"Robert Norwood-Díaz incorrectly informed you that Maya Norwood-Díaz was missing."

"I know she's not missing, but has he mentioned her again since?"

"He has not mentioned your mother again since," P-Body said. It paused for a moment, as if thinking about the question. "Before this evening, he had not spoken of your mother since last Tuesday, when he commented that he missed her macaroni and cheese at 4:34 PM."

Kristen smiled. "She made amazing mac."

She checked the kitchen. It was tidy, save for a half-full mug of coffee on the table. It reminded her of growing up. The house was always full of half-filled cups he left around. It seemed he had yet to break the habit.

Kristen sniffed the mug's contents. As she'd expected, there was a hint of Irish cream in it. She took a sip, regretted drinking the room-temperature coffee immediately, and dumped it into the sink.

"P, I need you to stop spiking Dad's drinks."

"Robert Norwood-Díaz adds liquor to his own drinks. When I suggest he abstain, he becomes mildly combative. Robert Norwood-Díaz does not listen to my suggestions regarding his health eighty-seven percent of the time."

"That sounds right. Where is he?"

P-Body's eye flickered, then came back just as bright as before.

"Robert Norwood-Díaz is resting in his bedroom. He arrived there—"

"Thanks, P."

Dad was not resting. When Kristi approached his open door, he was seated in front of Mom's old mirror, neck twisted, hands fussing with the external memory affixed to the side of his head. Dad had opened the mod up, pried open a panel, and revealed a mess of wires and silicon, his fingers reaching in and removing a piece.

"Dad, what the hell are you doing?" she asked.

"Hey, Kristi," Dad said. The way he responded was as if she'd just commented on the weather, rather than watching him dissect his own memory. He hardly glanced at her, just winced as he stared down at the metallic shard he'd pulled from his exmem. "P-Body says I called you earlier."

"Put that back."

"*That* is why I called you. And—you'll think this is funny—I don't remember calling anyone."

"Hilarious. Maybe you'll remember when you put that shard back in, hm? What are you thinking? How did you even get that panel off? They're not designed to be tinkered with like this, especially by an English teacher."

He let his hands fall to his lap, leaving his exmem exposed, and adjusted his wheelchair so that he could face her. His lips were drawn in a tight, subtle frown. "I don't remember the call because my memory shorted. The piece I just removed was damaged."

"It shorted?"

He nodded. "It started to recall old memories without command. For a moment, I was my younger self, sometimes before Mom. Sometimes I remembered things after her. I'm not sure, exactly. I told P-Body to share only what it felt was necessary for me to know. I imagine all those old memories, convinced they were in a younger body, were in for a shock when they discovered what we'd become." Dad smiled sadly and tapped the arm of his wheelchair. "The bot can keep that horror show to itself."

"You're okay now, though?"

"I certainly hope so. P turned it off and helped me open this damned thing so I could remove this—I think it's what caused the short. Not sure what caused the shard to break, though. Or if it will happen again."

Kristen held out her hand. "Give that to me. I know somebody at the hospital who can take a look at it. Maybe they can see what happened."

"Okay." He put the shard into her palm.

A typical shard was larger and had a grip on the end so a person could easily insert and remove it from whatever ports they had on their computer, tablet, or body. This one was specialized for mods like Dad's external memory. It was smaller, thinner, and lacked any kind of grip, almost like a piece of paper. Whatever had happened cracked it halfway down the middle, and it looked charred. Kristen looked into the cavity of Dad's exposed exmem. She convinced him to let her hold a light to the mod and took a picture of it with her lens. This was far out of her area of expertise—she was a biological surgeon—but she understood enough to know that something looked wrong.

Kristen sat on the bed and talked with her father for a while. She wanted to observe him for a bit longer and make sure he wasn't on the verge of a relapse—if an exmem glitch could relapse. He apologized for frightening her. She changed the subject and asked what he was reading lately. He lost himself explaining an old memoir about some early twenty-first century tycoon and all the insane things they got involved with. None of it sounded real, but she didn't interrupt. He didn't seem to have any trouble remembering the book or telling her about it. He didn't shout for her dead mother. Progress.

After she was satisfied that her father was out of the woods, at least for the night, Kristen announced that she should get on the road. "I have work in the morning. Keep that thing off for now and you should be fine, but give me a call if you need anything at all. I'll grab something from the hospital if you need it and head on over."

"Are you allowed to do that?" he asked.

Kristen shrugged. "You think they'll stop me?"

He smiled a toothy grin. "They wouldn't dare. Well, I'm glad you stopped by. Sorry it was under these circumstances."

"You kidding? I got a present." Kristen held up his damaged shard.

"Message me if anything like this happens again," Kristen told P-Body. They were in the entryway, far from Dad's bedroom, but she still spoke in hushed tones.

"You may want to know that Robert Norwood-Díaz has been having trouble remembering things lately. His use of his external memory bank has increased gradually over the last year, with more significant increases in the last month."

"Keep your voice down. Good to know, though. So, it's not just old memories of Mom backfiring?"

"Robert Norwood-Díaz has begun expressing problems with memory retention, but this is the first instance of his modified Horizon Mnemonic model mike-two-four—"

"First time his exmem broke."

"Correct. This evening's incident was new, but related. A variety of factors may cause the underlying issues: out-of-date software, corrupted programming, or damaged hardware. It may also be a sign of extreme stress, overuse of alcohol, an issue with one of his implants, hydrocephalus, or an early sign of Alzheimer's disease or another form of dementia."

"He doesn't drink enough for it to be alcoholism, and he's too retired to be stressed. Shouldn't be a compatibility issue, either. Not much chrome in his system. Stubborn bastard couldn't even be bothered to repair his legs."

"His external memory bank malfunctioning may lead to more severe issues, considering the way that it is hardwired into his temporal lobe. When its panel was removed, we had to disable it. Robert Norwood-Díaz's external memory will remain disabled until an engineer turns it back on."

"Good, make sure he keeps it turned off for now."

"My directive is to serve Robert Norwood-Díaz. I cannot employ the use of force unless he specifically instructs me and it is within the confines of SyncLair Robotics' terms of use. If you would like to—"

"Just... Just keep an eye on him, P. That's all I need from you right now."

Armani was in the hospital cafeteria, dressed in a pair of black scrubs. Her curly hair was pulled back, her edges smooth and regal. She sat across from a woman Kristen didn't recognize. She was a few years older than Armani, dressed in street clothes, with a visitor's pass around her neck. Circuitry was installed under the skin around her eyes, working its way toward her temples. Her blond hair was shaved along her right side—to make room for more mods—and neck-length on the left. Her body was shaped like a model's, and pink glow wire wove around her left arm. When Kristen stopped in front of them, the visitor glanced up at her with bright pink irises.

"Hey," Kristen interrupted their conversation. "I'm so sorry. Do you mind if I borrow Armani from you for a sec? I've got an engineering question for her."

"I'm on break," Armani said flatly.

"Sorry, it's important. I just—"

"One of your patients' mods are acting up?" the visitor asked.

"My Dad, actually. He's acting like it's nothing, but—"

"It's never nothing," the woman smiled, speaking quickly. She extended a hand, revealing an array of mods along her right arm that Kristen didn't recognize. Armani glanced away from them in a huff. "I'm Alis. I'm an engineer too, and Armani's wife."

"Fiancée," Armani corrected as the two of them shook hands.

"Details," Alis chuckled. "Sit down. I'm so bored. Got used to being in Toronto, where I was constantly being pulled in all directions. Then the move. But now, everything is mostly put away and I'm just waiting on the office here to process my paperwork."

"Don't hold your breath on them," Kristen said, taking the offered seat beside Armani. "So, does that mean we'll be working together soon? My name's Kristen, it's nice to meet you. I didn't know Armani had a *wife*."

Armani grunted through a bottle of orange juice.

"I got a ring and everything," Alis said, splaying out her fingers. One of them had a diamond strapped to it. The stone looked expensive. "But you still need to tell us what's going on with your dad."

Kristen explained the situation with her father as concisely as she could. Alis was rapt with attention throughout, asking questions about her father's use of his external memory, the model he used, year of installation, and all other kinds of questions Kristen couldn't quite answer. Even Armani began to chime in once she showed them the cracked and blackened shard Dad removed.

Alis whistled at it. "He really ruined his mem, didn't he?"

"It's good that his bot turned it off," Armani added. "If that thing did *this* to the hardware, only a matter of time before it affected your Dad's organics."

"So, he should get it removed?" Kristen asked.

"Right away," Armani said. "Get him to book an appointment with his clinic."

"He got it from some old shop downtown. They aren't in business anymore."

"Shit, and walk-ins take months to get seen."

"Months?" Alis asked.

"More demand for mods than there are clinics here," Armani explained. "Lots of people travel out of Knox to get an installation."

Alis nodded. "I traveled for some of mine, but only because I grew up in the middle of nowhere. My local clinic only did low-impact installations. Touch-ups, software updates, and a little glow wear," she said, and the pink wiring in her arm flashed at them. "I think they might be doing light tattoos now, but even that was off the table back then."

"I'll make some calls, then," Kristen said. "Maybe I'll get lucky."

"Why don't you just let me have a look?" Alis said.

Kristen blinked at her.

"What? I've got nothing to do but sit around and wait for Mani to get done working. This'll be fun! I haven't done a house call in *years*. Besides, clinics are in it for the money. There are good ones out there, but they're hard to come by."

Kristen glanced over at Armani and sent her a message: *[11:25] Is she for real?*

A flash of white appeared over Armani's eye. She blinked it away just as quickly and said, "Don't be fooled by the way the office is dragging their feet. Alis used to consult for them, then fly back to Canada when she was done. Back and forth. Then they stole her. Toronto's still pissed about it. She's one of the best medi-engies out there. If she wants to do a house call, you'd be a fool to turn her down."

Alis reached out and took Armani's hand. "Moving here was an easy choice to make."

"Although," Armani squeezed her hand back, "I don't get why she can't just fucking *relax*. Ally will never get this much time off again until she retires or dies. I wish she'd just chill out for one second."

"I relaxed for the first few days," Alis said, digging her nails into Armani's palm. "Today, I'm making a house call."

"My break ends in a minute," Kristen said. "I just took fifteen to come talk with Armani and—"

"When are you done? Maybe we can go see your dad after."

"Three."

Alis grinned at Armani. "This *afternoon,* I'm making a house call."

Armani laughed from her chest.

"Thank you," Kristen said.

Alis smiled. "Of course," she said, as if they were old friends.

Alis waited for Kristen in the air-conditioned hospital lobby at 3:00 PM. At some point between lunch and then, she had returned home to get her things: two gym bags stuffed to the brim with tools and monitors. They threw the bags into Kristen's car and drove to Dandridge.

The map on Kristen's lens showed that traffic was backed up on I-40, so she took the long way around. Alis tried to kill time by asking questions about her dad and his mods. Kristen still didn't have the answers she needed, though, and a silence soon filled the car. Kristen broke it by asking about Toronto, and Alis told her about the "glitch ward" at her old hospital. She talked about patients with rebel mods, divers dissociating from reality, and victims of hacking, some left in comas. She seemed genuinely excited by all of it at times.

"You ever see anything like what I showed you earlier? The broken shard?" Kristen asked as they neared the exit for Dandridge. "Any idea why it broke?"

"I'm not sure. I've got some suspicions. Lots of mods go bad because of cheap tech. Clinics look to undercut each other as much as they compete for the most cutting-edge mods, and their clients always suffer for it, whether from cheap implants or untested ones. Sometimes nothing goes wrong, and that's great, but if your father wasn't the victim of a hack or involved with some gang fight—"

Kristen laughed. "He's a retired English teacher."

"Hey, you can't trust English teachers."

Kristen caught a glimpse of Alis' smile out of the corner of her eye.

Alis continued, "But I'm thinking that the clinic who gave your father his external memory cut corners of some kind. Won't know for sure until I see it close up, though."

Dad flicked on an old standing lamp, tilting it on its base to reach the switch. Its bulb cast a pale-yellow glow around the living room.

The introductions were brief. Alis was eager to see Dad's external memory. He offered to pry it open, as he had the prior day, but Alis was already retrieving a small screwdriver from one of the bags she'd brought. She pressed it to the mod and turned, eventually discarding the tool for another. Dad did his best to keep his head still as she worked, but Alis didn't make it easy. When he complained that she was pressing too hard, she accused him of mangling his exmem.

"P-Body's the one that opened me up," Dad said.

Alis' eyes flicked to the bot standing in the corner of the room, then back to her work. "Don't you blame your problems on them. They're programmed to take out the trash and call you an ambulance; it's not their fault that they're not equipped for medical engineering."

Alis got into Dad's exmem after a few minutes of working at the metal casing. It popped off the side of his head, exposing the charred circuitry and silicon inside. Kristen watched Alis' face snap from surprise to curiosity, her lips ajar and a neon glint in her eyes. She hadn't noticed it before, but now that her eyes were alight, it was impossible to tell if Alis was wearing advanced lenses or had installed some incredibly realistic optic implants.

Kristen took a seat across from them as Alis clamped a device to the mod's guts. She watched its screen for a moment, made a small humming noise, then replaced the device with another. She conducted several of these tests without a word, her lips contorting and her eyes flickering—the way P-Body's eye did when it was processing something.

Alis used a pair of needle-nose pliers to remove another shard from the exmem and held it under the light, flipping it over. It looked different from the one he'd given her the other day. It was longer, with jagged tendrils on one end, looking almost like a weed plucked from the ground, roots and all.

"This is an LN07-M," Alis said.

Dad turned to look at Alis.

"Sorry. You don't need to know that. The important thing is that the shard you showed me, Kristen, was *not* the same kind. It wasn't even the same company. This is by Laopo-Ng, made in Vietnam. The one that got charred the other day was made by Traveler Technologies, of U.S. make. Both are fine to use. Lao is actually pretty good, though they've fallen out of style recently due to some outdated software, but still totally fine for a budget mod.

"The problem is putting two brands together, and this is a really odd combo. They don't even speak the same language—I don't mean the people, I mean the way the code's written. To even attempt it, you'd need to hack the shards and fool one into thinking it was the same as the other. Trick the Traveler into thinking it's another Lao, for example. However, that would still cause the wearer a great deal of discomfort, you know? It *works*, but the wearer would have headaches when they're using local memories. Searing pain any time they accessed the exmem."

"It's been fine until just recently," Dad said, staring at the opposite wall.

"Exactly. You'd need a way to remove the pain, wouldn't you? Whoever installed this bad boy had a business to run. I've seen plenty of rigged mods that worked totally fine. However, this looks like a rush job—getting stock out the door before the feds come sniffing around. I saw it all the time in Toronto. That's why they added this little beauty into the mix." Alis tapped on Dad's exmem with her pliers. He winced at it. "Kristen, come look at this. You ever see one of these little guys in a mod during surgery? Maybe you helped to install a few. The red and white dongle, there."

Kristen leaned forward and peered into the cavity of Dad's exmem. She recognized the part right away.

"Yeah, we go through a few each week. Amputees get the largest ones," she said.

"You know why?" Alis grinned.

"They block the pain, help the patient ease into—"

"So, why does Mr. Norwood-Díaz have one in his still-at-tached head? Good question. The surgeon who installed this must have known that they couldn't get away with tossing their hacked exmem on anyone. They'd be outed immediately. So they added a nociception editor. You might have heard it called a pain blocker, or bouncer—one kid I treated told me it was a *superman*."

"Shit," Kristen muttered.

"I know. Blood clinics are really getting good with market-ing this junk."

"That's not—"

"I know, I'm sorry."

"So take it out," Dad said, arms folded over his chest. "Not just the no-see—whatever you called it. The external memory. It's already damaged. I've probably lost everything stored in there, anyway."

"Ideally, I would agree with you," Alis said, grimacing at the mod, the tip of her pliers pressed against her cheek. Her eyes flickered and shifted, her gaze fixated on Dad's exmem. "I'm not sure I can remove it, and not just because we're doing a little living room surgery. I mean that I'm not sure *anyone* can rip that."

"Why not?" Kristen asked.

"Look, whatever happened the other day, it fried the editor. That caused a chain reaction which burnt the shards—and all of that is hard-wired into your dad's head. We're talking about the organic skull and grey matter here. Stuff we can't engineer. Well, we *can*, but that's experimental tech and unless you're Platinum Premium...

"Sorry, I got off track again. Mani says I do that too much. I was talking about the organics. Those connections in his brain got fried, too. If we remove them, you're risking damaging his local memories. Everything that's stored the old-fashioned way. Even if the surgery was a success, he might not make it out intact. Best case, you lose some memories of that dog your parents had, the city you visited in '29, or of little Kristen growing up. Worst case, well, I'd highly recommend you make sure your affairs are in order first."

Dad sighed heavily and slumped into his chair. He stared down at his hands, jaw slack, picking at his nails and flicking away specks of dirt that had accumulated. Or, perhaps he was just going through the motions, remembering when he worked on an old neighbor's farm when he was still in high school, or about the time he and Mom took Kristen to the beach.

The first time Kristen set eyes on the Atlantic Ocean was on her twelfth birthday, when Mom and Dad took her to Chocowinity, North Carolina. It was a long, cramped, seven-hour drive. Kristen remembered being disappointed that the beach was more mud than sand, and the ocean looked like a swamp. As far as she could see, the land gently dipped into the water, ruins of old towns and farms barely visible through the trees and reeds. Within minutes, Dad packed their things and drove down the peninsula to Minnesott Beach, a small bastion of sun and sand along the drowned coast. Kristen and Mom made a sandcastle, and Dad saw to the defenses, digging an absurdly deep mote. He'd insisted it would keep the waves from reaching the castle.

Most of Kristen's external storage was used for work, to help her memorize complicated surgeries and contingency plans should they ever go wrong. She couldn't imagine losing that—but Dad installed his in his twenties, when he was still living in Atlanta, before he'd met Mom or moved north. He'd practically spent a lifetime backing things up on it.

"I'm sorry," Alis said, timidly breaking the horrible silence that had fallen in Dad's living room. "If you keep the external memory off, you should be fine. At least, there probably won't be any additional damage. If you want, I can rewire it while I have the lid off anyway and prevent you from turning it on again. Just takes a sec. It won't be out of your head, but you won't turn it on by accident. Not without significant help, at least."

Dad looked at her. Bags hung under his eyes, and his jaw was slack. He shrugged in a way that said to her: *It's your call.*

"There's got to be something we can do to save some of the memories on there," Kristen said. "Not all of the memories, I'm sure, but if we take out the rest of the shards, maybe then we can salvage some."

"I'm not sure anything's left. The shard you showed me was cracked down the middle. This one's cooked. The rest don't look any better, and I don't like the idea of you walking around with a little bomb strapped to your head, Mr. Norwood-Díaz. Sorry if that's too graphic, but—"

"No, you're right," Dad said.

Kristen put a hand on Dad's shoulder. "Do it."

Over the following weeks, things went back to normal, for the most part. Alis disappeared into the hospital's labyrinthine halls. During a surgery that Kristen and Armani had together, she said Alis was busy working on some experimental projects involving biocompressors—beyond anything she understood, but it seemed important. Sometimes they saw each other in the cafeteria, but Alis took most of her meals to her office.

Kristen's life once again revolved around the hospital, and she continued to transcribe old books for Clingman's Press in her rare moments of free time. She finished the thriller she'd been working on and began an old romance novel she'd found from the early 2000s. It was cheesy and terrible, but in the kind of way that made her reluctant to put the book down.

At night, Kristen found she often needed melatonin to sleep, in a way that she hadn't *needed* it since med school.

She visited her father every weekend after his exmem burned, picking up takeout from the No. 1 Chinese restaurant on the way. They took turns picking movies to watch.

When Tomas joined her, they cooked together in Dad's kitchen. Kristen didn't enjoy cooking, but after a while, she found that she did like using Dad's big French kitchen knives. He taught her to use them, how to tuck her fingers and rock the blade back and forth. Tomas started calling her his sous-chef, and she liked that too.

Most importantly, she could tell Dad looked forward to helping prepare whatever was on the menu each night. Tomas came ready with a new recipe each time. Sometimes, they were incredible. Others, like the tikka masala, never came out quite right. Among the three of them, nobody could figure out how to make that sauce, which was maddening because it really didn't look that difficult. They handed the duty off to P-Body as a joke, but the bot took its job seriously, and it did a better job than any of them. P-Body was in charge of mixing all of the sauces from then on, and each time they cooked together, it asked if they needed one.

One evening, Tomas brought ingredients to make sierra en escabeche—pickled fish. It was something Dad mentioned once, a hint of a memory from a dinner he and Mom once shared. Tomas hadn't been able to get real fish, but the tofu substitute was on its fourth day of marinating in oil, vinegar, and at least a dozen spices. The dish took a few hours to prepare, despite the fact Tomas had cooked the tofu before marinating it. Kristen was ravenous by the time he plated it. They could have made tacos, and she would have been just as happy, but Dad said it was the best thing he'd tasted all year. When she finally took a bite, Kristen suspected he might be right.

"There had better be more of this," she told Tomas through a half-full mouth.

Tomas just smiled and shrugged. "It's a little salty. I think I could balance the flavors a bit better next time. Maybe let it marinate for another day to let them soak in more. Or maybe I just need to find some actual fish."

"You marry that man," Dad said, tapping her on the shoulder, a wide toothy grin spread across his face. "You marry him right now, or I will."

As the summer waned, Dad began to clean up around the house. P-Body helped him, but Kristen offered to lend a hand as well while she was visiting. She wound up in a nook off the kitchen, where Dad had set up a small library to house his books. Tall metal shelves lined the walls, each filled so full of books that some shelves had two rows. Some of the smaller ones sat on their sides on top of other books, while others had found a place on nearby end tables or Dad's desk in the center of the room. Many of them were stories she remembered reading as a child, though his collection had grown even more in the last few years. There were biographies, memoirs, poetry, and all manner of fiction. She found reprints whose pages looked untouched, and water-damaged titles dated as far back as the late twentieth century.

A pocketbook caught Kristen's eye: *The East Tennessee Birdwatcher's Guide*. It lay atop several books, a sheen of dust across its cover. It was Mom's, once. Of all people, Kristen never understood why her mother carried around a birding book. This was the same woman who threw knives to relax, and who once smuggled condoms into prison for a friend—allegedly. *That* woman was reading facts about the downy fucking woodpecker.

Kristen picked up the book and wiped the cover on her jeans, leaving a smear of grey dust behind. Without it, the book was rather pretty. Geese, songbirds, and a few others she didn't recognize were illustrated on it in lovely watercolors. She liked the orange bird with black wings, though she couldn't recall ever seeing one in the wild. Kristen checked the publication date: 2059.

Dad's wheels bumped over the seam in the doorway and came down on the other side. P-Body was just behind him, carrying a box half-full of things Dad had kept too long: clothes with holes in the seams, paper mail, and a broken mug from Dollywood. Kristen made a note through her lens and filed it away—*Dad, x-mas, Dolly mug.*

"Have you read that one?" Dad asked, nodding at the birding book in Kristen's hands.

"Nah. I pilfered your adventure books. Not this stuff."

He nodded. "Your mother once threatened to ground you because you wouldn't do anything but read *Percy Jackson.*"

"She did?"

"You don't remember that? I convinced her not to, but I'm certain you heard us arguing."

"I remember the book, but not that."

"Ah. Perhaps you were reading at the time. I know you're busier now, but there was a time when if you found a good book—a really good one—you may as well have been dead to the world."

Kristen flipped the birding book over in her hands. There were quotes on the back from names she didn't recognize and teasers about the information within, such as how the barn swallow indirectly led to the conservation movement in the

United States, apparently. She filed that away in her external memory, just in case it came in handy during trivia night at the Cantina.

"I wish I could port *Percy Jackson* for Clingmans," she said. "It would be fun to revisit that one. Share it with my friends."

"You can't?"

"I mean, I could, but I'd have a team of lawyers knocking on my door the moment they found out. It hasn't rolled over into the public domain yet, even though it should have."

"Ah, right. Well, what about that one?"

"Mom's birding book? Nobody would buy that."

"Kristi, you republish old books people have already forgotten about. If you were doing this for the money, you would never have gotten started in the first place."

She turned the book over again. The cover really was striking, and the text was in great condition—as she expected from her family. There was no sign of flood damage or missing pages, though its spine had worn down with age. Adapting the book for digital reading opened some interesting possibilities, too. Normally, she only dealt with text, but with that, she could display images of each bird alongside it. Or, if she could get her hands on some video of each bird that she could display on people's lenses, that could be even better. Kristen could advertise it as not just a relic of the past, but featuring the birds lost to time. Others had done things like that before, so she knew it was possible, but most of those books were about superheroes or dragons.

Even if it didn't sell, Dad was right. She wasn't making money on her other books, anyway. Maybe she'd come away with a better idea why Mom picked up birding toward the end. Worst-case scenario, maybe she'd discover a new love for the feathered creatures that used to dominate the skies. There were so many, once.

"Alright," Kristen said. "I'll do it."

Dad smiled. Even P-Body seemed to make some kind of light confirmation noise.

Dad said, "I don't think it's the legacy your mother would have expected—maybe not quite the one she'd want—but I'm glad a piece of what she loved will be saved."

"I'm still going to tell people about the shit she got into. This is just one legacy among many."

"One among many," he agreed. "That would make for a good dedication page."

Dad steered his chair under the desk and moved around some files. Many of them went into an old-school filing cabinet and others into the box P-Body carried. As he was cleaning up, Kristen noticed his old laptop was out, and he'd been making notes. He'd tucked a few written on yellow paper beneath the edge of his computer.

"What are you working on?" Kristen asked. "Are you writing again?"

He blushed. "It's silly."

"Tell me." She smiled.

"Your publishing venture reminded me of my own love of books, of writing. I used to have big dreams of being published one day when I was younger, you know."

"I remember you holing away in your old office on weekends and summers, typing so loud it filled the hall."

He chuckled. "Well, I started a few little projects around the time you kicked off Clingmans, but none of it went anywhere. I never felt like I found the *right* story to tell."

Dad stared down at his desk, brow furrowed.

Kristen said, "It's fine if you don't want to talk about it, I was—"

"No, you should know. Given recent events, I find it difficult to remember some things. I worry it will get worse. Maybe that's foolish, but I've lost so much in such a short time. I was…"

Dad scowled at the notes as he revealed them, in the way somebody might contort their face to avoid crying. The notes were written in his cat-scratch, so they were tough to read from where Kristen stood, but she caught a few names, places, and dates. Each harkened back to something they'd done as a family. Among them was one that read *Minnesott Beach, NC. 2133.*

"Dad..."

"I don't want to lose any more memories. Not of the things that matter. I was thinking about that and trying to figure out what to do with it. I know I can't undo what's been done, I can't fix anything, but maybe I can find another way to hold on to what's left. To record it. So, I've started making notes whenever I remember things about us. About you and your mother. I found the story I need to write, Kristen. It's your mother's."

"You're writing Mom's memoir."

He nodded. "She would think it was foolish, wouldn't she?"

Kristen laughed. "Yeah, probably. She'd tell you to go to the lake or something instead."

Dad laughed with her. "She did love that lake."

He paused for a moment, then found a pen and wrote on a piece of paper: *Douglas Lake, 2121.*

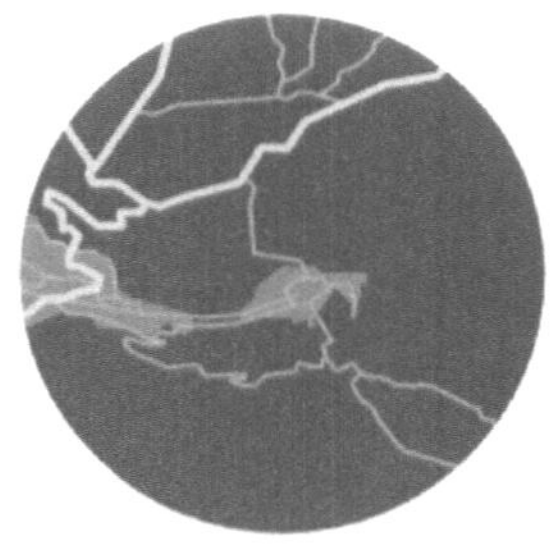

Fireworks Above the Badlands

Muro Etrusche & Civita di Bagnoregio, Italy — 2166

THE SUN CAST GOD rays through the window blinds as it set, illuminating the dust in the air. The office of De Campo Investigatori Privati was of two minds. David De Campo's desk was where he and his wife greeted clients. He cleaned it daily. His father—an old-fashioned New Yorker with a potent case of OCD—always said that a cluttered desk led to a cluttered mind. David heard that phrase enough that it proved true. Mafalda's desk, on the other hand, was a perpetual disaster. David's wife thought in terms of *stuff*: sticky notes and evidence mingled with half-drunk mugs of coffee and a bottle of allergy pills. Her laptop seemed an afterthought in comparison. Perhaps it was. She hardly used the old thing anymore.

David recently purchased a divider to hide his wife's clutter from their clients. It was made of bamboo and steel, giving their little home office the guise of looking rather distinguished. With a little wall art and paint—something with a bit of warmth—they came dangerously close to a livable place.

The doorbell buzzed. Its harsh tone filled the office, and a notification flashed in the corner of David's vision. He set his toolbox behind the divider and went to the door.

David led Mr. and Mrs. Segreti into the office. The time was 16:57 PM, two days before the new year, and two days since they'd last heard from their son. Mr. Segreti laid out the situation: their son, Ennio, had slept over at his friend Vanni's house two nights prior. They lived within a couple of blocks of each other in Calanchi, a neighborhood off the eastern façade, the kind of place with private pools and trimmed hedges. Calanchi residents got robbed from time to time, but it was rare to hear about anyone going missing out there. When they did, a demand for ransom usually arrived no less than twenty-four hours later. So far, that didn't seem to be Ennio's case.

Mr. Segreti called Ennio when he hadn't come home the following day. He had apparently left his friend's that morning—about seven hours before the Segretis rang David's doorbell. They asked around for Ennio in the time between, tried the boy's comms, and got nothing for it.

Ennio's mother added some context: the boy never went anywhere on a whim. During a recent trip to visit her sister in Fonteblanda, he'd expressed interest in the beach. He only took it upon himself to visit it when it became clear that nobody had the time to bring him. Ennio loved the smell of the sea, she said, and lamented the fact that they lived so far from water. David suppressed a smile. The closest body of water was Lago di Bolsena. Public transport ran that way sparingly, and it was a long trek any other way, especially for a nine-year-old boy.

The Fonteblanda incident wasn't the only case of Ennio sneaking off on his own. Mrs. Segreti went to Switzerland recently on business and took the family along. While she was in a work meeting, Ennio found his way on the path up Drunengalm. The mountain had been featured as a set piece for the 2131 *Lord of the Rings* film. The boy had taste—that movie was a classic. Apparently, Ennio had wanted to walk the same peaks as the Fellowship, but only made it partway before he found his way back down and returned to the hotel. That wasn't a surprise. The Alps were no joke. Seasoned hikers had trouble scaling them, and David was fairly certain that the actor who played the 2131 Aragorn sprained an ankle on Drunengalm while they were filming that sequence.

To complicate things, Ennio was partially deaf, walking around with a fresh new cochlear implant to help his hearing—among other things, no doubt. Cochlear implants had graduated over the years into something like a Swiss army knife. They were excellent for hands-free calls, had shard ports, integrated with one's lenses or optics, and more. David and his wife both used them. Ennio's father seemed to suggest that the implant would sell well if a scrapper got his hands on the boy, but couldn't bring himself to say the words. Instead he just repeated how new and expensive it was.

Mrs. Segreti was certain he'd just wandered off but couldn't imagine where in the city he might have gone. He sought adventures, but he'd already been everywhere in Muro Etrusche.

"Perhaps the civita caught his eye?" David suggested.

Civita di Bagnoregio was an old Etruscan town founded sometime around 470 BCE. Every stone had been restored or replaced since then, but one could still walk through the Porta San Maria and visit Antica Civitas or Chiesa di San Donato. Every morning, Padre Nicolí held mass in that ancient cathedral. If one could block out the sound of the city below, the place was a living, breathing time capsule of a town—one that shouldn't exist.

The old village was built upon a hill of tuff and clay. It was a brilliant, easily defensible position for the Etruscans, but the years had not been kind to it. The hill was constantly eroding, falling out from beneath the civita. Hundreds of buildings, ancient homes and shops, lay in the ground below (or were taken to museums throughout Italy). What was left only existed because of the great wall surrounding the remnants of the old hill. That was the city's purpose. Muro Etrusche was built around the civita to preserve what remained of it. Everything in the city revolved around the massive retaining walls that kept the hill from spilling out from beneath the civita. That impermanence made the town a tourist trap, which had greatly contributed both to the town's decline and funding its restoration.

Despite everything, Civita di Bagnoregio was still dying. The city was working on a project to suspend the ruins on an artificial floor, removing the need for the hill rather than preventing it from eroding, but funding had become an issue in recent years. The money went to securing freshwater interests, WEUSF flood and wildfire relief, or funding their allies' wars. All of that inevitably led to political gridlock and in-fighting, no matter the outcome. Lately, there was talk of scrapping the preservation project altogether and moving what they could to the Museo Nazionale in Rome before the civita collapsed in on itself.

Ennio's father shook his head. He didn't seem to buy the idea that Ennio had gone to the civita.

His mother spoke in Italian, her words translated on David's heads-up display. He knew the language well enough that he didn't need captions most of the time, but they made him more confident that he wasn't misinterpreting the native speakers. "[Ennio has been to Civita di Bagnoregio many times. He knows its streets like the back of his hand. It's not a good adventure to him anymore, it's just an old neighborhood in the city.]"

"But I cannot imagine what else he would go," the father said in broken English. He sighed, as though the admission had taken something from him. "There's nothing else in the city that might interest him. He loves classic adventures through the wilderness, and there's no mountain to climb or lake to swim in."

"The valley has many hills and plateaus," David suggested.

"It is possible," the father said. "[But I don't think the Badlands are enough for Ennio. He fancies himself a real adventurer. He talks about Marco Polo and that Norwegian who sailed the Northwest.]"

"Roald Amundsen," his wife said.

"Ah. You see, [Mister] De Campo, hills are nothing to [my son. He is not a normal boy.]"

"Alright," David said, trying his best to sound hopeful. Ennio's case seemed like it would be a challenge. There were so few leads. Still, he knew enough to get started. That, plus enough cameras and a little help from the Net, might be enough. "I'll do my best to find your son. I'll be in touch by the new year."

"That soon?"

"I'll be in touch, Signore Segreti," David repeated.

There was a lot of city to cover and not a lot of time. Unless Ennio was with somebody, or had taken to thievery, the boy may already be in need of food and water. His parents discovered he was missing that morning, but who was to say he didn't sneak off in the night—or the day before when he was supposed to be at his friend's house? It wouldn't be the first time a kid used a sleepover as an excuse to slip away. Hopefully he packed snacks.

David made a call to the police station and asked for Detective Quintino Kimedi, an old friend from the second West Coast War. Quintino had been part of a small task force Italy deployed to assist them in California in 2158. They hadn't worked together for long, but he was one of the few close friends David had found since moving from Upper New York to Muro Etrusche.

The station found Quintino after a few minutes. After a quick chat, the detective conducted a search for Ennio Segreti, but their systems didn't pull anything up. The last time they caught him on camera was two days prior, at the address where he'd spent the night with his friend.

"Dammit," David said. "Do me a favor and keep the query going for me, will you, Quinn?"

"Tsk. Davey, you know I will, [but you need to get yourself an access point one of these days. One that *I* don't need to be involved with.] If the fellas upstairs hear you and Maf are leaning on us still, they're going to come down hard on that private practice of yours."

"Or they'll try to hire us."

Quintino laughed. "They too petty for that."

"That's not how the scandal in Bagnoregio Commune went down. Practically begged for our help."

"They was in a tough spot, you know that. And they were sour that they had to rely on outsiders for that case. An *American*, at that."

"The horror," David said, grinning.

"[Next time they won't be breaking bread with you two, if you get my meaning.]"

"Then keep it hush-hush. Ping me if anything turns up."

"Okay. [Don't work too hard, Davey. We're expecting you and Maf for the New Year fireworks. We rented out a section of the wall, and there's this balcony looking over the south end—you'll love it.] There will be so many explosions, it'll feel just like you're back in [the United States]."

"Well when you put it like that, I guess we'll be there."

"[You had better. All these favors you're calling in, and I haven't gotten to beat your ass in cards since last summer. There's something not right about that.]"

David grinned. "I've been playing with Maf. I think I'll give you a run for your money this year."

"Tsk. Make sure to polish your fingers before you come," Quintino said. David could hear a faint clicking in the background. The policeman was tapping a metal-tipped finger against his desk. "[I don't want any excuses about how your wallet isn't working when you inevitably lose your shirt.]"

David tried the bus garage next. They had cameras installed in their vehicles and at the stations. Some of their networks were off the police's grid—a detail that had been a recurring point of contention between the two for years. David cared little, so long as he got access to their feeds. If Ennio boarded a bus anywhere in the country, they would have picked it up.

When nobody answered his call at the city center, David grabbed his coat, turned off the neon *Investigatori Privati* sign in the window, and stepped onto the sidewalk of Via Sud. The street stretched out along the southern façade, lined on each side by a tangle of steel and stone, all of it encapsulated by an entropic neon glow—the colors mingling above the asphalt. The tallest buildings faded into the massive wall that propped up Civita di Bagnoregio above, a dusting of snow along their rooftops. Below, most of it had become muddy puddles and slush.

The nearest bus station was just down the street, a few blocks eastward. David walked through the front door at a rapid pace, eager to arrive before the office closed for the evening. The woman behind the counter glanced up at him over her monitor. Her eyes were distant and unfocused, like she had already clocked out for the year.

When David asked about access to their surveillance system, she gave a canned response and refused to forward the call or message to anyone else. She didn't seem to care much that a child was missing.

David left the garage empty-handed, a bitter taste in his mouth. A few years back, he could have gotten what he needed. If the army hadn't disabled his military-grade chrome, he might have been able to hack into their systems himself, but since he left active service, he couldn't hack a toaster. All they'd left him with were the things that had slipped onto the public market: a dermal wrap that turned his skin into light armor and a pair of Edison "Oracle" optics. Everything else was removed or disabled. He missed how easy it was to hack things the way he used to, but at least they'd let him keep his eyes. They'd turned out quite useful in the years since.

It was rush hour in the streets of Muro Etrusche. Every car, bus, and motorcycle competed to press forward through the morass the streets had become. David watched the steel river flow for a while before deciding to check on some houses around Calanchi. It was unlikely that anyone there knew Ennio's whereabouts, but perhaps they could point him in the right direction. Either way, there was one place he wanted to visit quite badly.

David walked from the bus station, keeping his pace brisk, and reached the house shortly after sundown. It was a small, single-family home with a garage larger than most inner-city apartments. A woman was unloading groceries from her car as he approached.

"Buonasera, signorina," David said as he made his way toward her, making sure that she saw and heard him approach. "Do you need help with those?"

"Uh, sure," she said. "[Thank you.]"

David picked up a heavy green bag that she pointed at. It was filled with nutrition bars, bricks of tofu, and a few bags of frozen fruit. They walked into the house. The door led into a small, cream-colored kitchen littered with pots, pans, and tomato stains. Her spice rack was out in the open, filling the air with a confusing mix of odors from oregano to garam masala.

"I'm sorry for the mess," the woman said, setting down her bags. "[Thank you, Mister.]"

David set the bag she'd given him beside the others. "No problem," he said.

"My name is Pia. You are the American who just moved into Nicolao's old place? You have a little bit of a New York accent, I can tell."

"Oh, no, I'm actually just in town looking for somebody. The Segreti family lives close to here, don't they?" David asked, knowing their house was exactly half a kilometer down the road. He flashed his private investigator license and said, "I run a small agency down in the city. The family came seeking help. Their boy, Ennio, he's gone missing."

Pia put a hand to her chest. "[My God.]"

At David's suggestion, Pia called her son down to the kitchen. She and Vanni had just seen Ennio the other day. They told him about how the boy had spent the night, which Pia indicated happened regularly. Apparently, the two boys were very close. However, when David asked where Ennio might have gone, Vanni shrugged and muttered something in Italian too quiet for David's ears or optics to relay a translation. His mother dismissed it, insisting her son was just upset by the news, but David suspected something else was afoot. Still, he wasn't prepared to force information out of the boy, not until he had something more concrete. He left his contact with Pia and told her to reach out if either of them remembered something about where Ennio might have gone.

"Give your son a little time to digest the news," David suggested as he stepped through the doorway. "This evening, or tomorrow, try to talk with him again, and let me know what he says."

"Vanni said he didn't know anything, [Mister.]"

"I know. But like you said, he's a bit rattled. Poor boy just found out one of his best friends is missing. Maybe something'll come to him. If not... Poor Ennio has already been missing for at least a day." David shrugged.

"Of course, I understand. Good luck, [Mister.]"

After David left, he messaged Quintino: *[18:10] Keep an eye on this address for me, too, will you?*

David knocked on doors in the neighborhood until the winter winds bit through his coat and threatened to render him numb. He hadn't learned anything new, but he'd made dozens of Ennio's neighbors aware of the situation. They could be his eyes and ears on Calanchi gossip, and if the boy made contact with anyone, it'd likely be one of his neighbors. If need be, he may be able to use that. If the boy remained missing for long enough, David might need to get creative and find a way to lure Ennio out.

That was assuming he'd run away, rather than the alternative.

As David began walking back home, he received a message from Mafalda: *[19:05] Can you meet me at Madonna's Bend? I could use your eyes on something.*

David checked a map through his optics, and a neon blue road map appeared over his view of the street. Just as he thought, the Bend wasn't far.

[19:05] Be there in twenty, he told his wife.

[19:07] Thanks. If you beat me there, don't go in without me.

[19:08] Into what?

She didn't respond. David checked the map again to see if there was another place called Madonna's Bend, but nothing came up. It didn't make sense. Madonna's Bend was a part of the wall around the civita. There were a few apartments and offices attached to it, and a fountain in the square below, but the Bend *itself* was just a wall. There wasn't anything to go into.

Skyscrapers clung to the massive walls surrounding Civita di Bagnoregio like barnacles on a ship. Skyways connected them high above the streets. Between the apartments, offices, and convenience stores along the wall, some of the people up there never had to touch the ground. Many along the eastern façade appeared to be constructed of what looked like heavy modular components stacked atop one another. Several bore large screens near ground level, advertising all manner of fashion, seafood, ramen, adult films, premium Antarctic water, mods that would make the wearer more attractive / powerful / happy, and dozens of ads for the 2068 series of cars and robotic attendants. Most of the text and audio were in Italian, but there were smatterings of English, French, Norwegian, and Japanese as well. The scene was nothing compared to what David had grown numb to in the States, but it was a *lot* for Italy.

Muro Etrusche lacked many of the restrictions the old Italian cities had. Rumor was, the wall around which the city was built had been bankrolled in large part by Pepsi-Pata and Norske Oseaniske Løsninger. They were likely just a few among many donors, though, given the collage of consumerism on display.

Madonna's Bend was a small stretch of the wall on the edge of the brightly lit eastern façade near the Madonna and Poeta apartment buildings, each of which housed some ten thousand people. David checked his messages again to see if Mafalda had said where exactly they should meet, but she hadn't responded. He decided to split the difference and wait in the well-lit alley between the two buildings. Something caught his eye as he approached it. There was a breach in the wall. David didn't think he would have noticed it if he hadn't been looking for something to *go into*, but it was certainly there: a wide crack nestled among the metal façade between the Madonna and Poeta. A police pylon was set in a patch of earth next to it, displaying in small, dimly glowing red font *Police Line: Do Not Cross*, almost as if even the police didn't want to draw attention to the place either.

Mafalda arrived a few minutes later. Her hair was pulled back into a bun, a pleather jacket draped over her shoulders, and a light tattoo on her neck displayed a pair of kanji characters shining yellow against her collar. Two enforcers followed her, each decked out in light and chrome. Some of their mods looked military grade. David spotted seams in their arms that likely concealed blades under the surface, and circuitry around their heads that suggested they had some quality neural mods. Each carried a pistol on their hips as well.

"[What's up?]" Mafalda asked, relaxed.

"Ciao," David said. "Who're your friends?"

"Gennoveffa [and] Jun'ichi," the woman behind Mafalda said, gesturing toward her partner as she said his name.

Jun'ichi gave David a slight nod, his eyes flaring an unnatural orange color as they caught the glow of the streetlight. He rolled up the sleeve of his puffy jacket and flashed a light tattoo: a glowing orange tiger baring fangs like bullets.

[19:31] You're working with the Tigres? David asked Mafalda in text.

A flash of blue appeared over Mafalda's eyes as she received and blinked the message away. She responded audibly, "Remember that case I was working on? The old woman who asked us to find her brother, the clinic surgeon?"

"Hachirō."

"Right. Well, it turns out the Tigres are also looking for him. They outbid her and are helping with the case now."

"Enforcers are only good for breaking things, not finding people. No offense, of course."

Gennoveffa wrinkled her nose at him.

"Hachirō is involved with worse crowds than we were led to believe, [love]. I'm talking about scavengers, eco-punks, the Rivoluzionari. I'm still figuring out the details but our new friends are just here to make sure that nobody ices me while I'm poking into their business. After all, if that happens, the Tigres don't get what they're looking for."

"Hachirō."

"Yes again," Gennoveffa said, smiling. "Also, the money he stole from Mama Cinzia."

David whistled.

"We can talk about this more later," Mafalda said. "For now, I want to check out this breach in the wall."

"It's connected to your case?"

"I think so," Mafalda said, walking past him toward the breach. She reached out and pried open the jagged slab of metal just enough to peer through. "It was a Tigres safehouse for years, until the—"

"The Rivoluzionari took it," David said. A set of colored rags had caught his eye, barely visible through the entrance into the wall. The radicals bore no logo or flag, but they used colored cloth to communicate silently in analog. It was impossible to trace in the Net, since it didn't exist there, and to interpret it in the Real you had to know the cypher. David didn't know what their codes meant, but he knew a Rivoluzionari signal when he saw one.

"They did," Gennoveffa said. "Although the idea that they 'took it' from us is generous. We had already abandoned the place. It became too well-known in the neighborhood. Kids snuck in on dares, and without a second entrance, it was too easy to get stuck inside. Anyone in there is also *stuck* in there."

"[It is a shit safehouse,]" Jun'ichi said in Japanese.

Gennoveffa sneered. "Mama Cinzia was grateful to be rid of the place."

"Let's have a look at it," Mafalda said.

She peeled back the metal sheet covering the entrance, filling the alley with an audible groan. As they stepped inside—except for Jun'ichi, who kept watch in the alley—their lenses adapted to the darkness. David's optics, courtesy of the U.S. government's deeming night vision and infrared were acceptable for public use, illuminated the space a bit more clearly. These helped him see his surroundings, and his HUD informed him of two other things: a drop in the temperature and humidity and his signal strength transitioning from strong to weak.

The old safehouse was narrow enough that David could reach the back of the wall and the breach itself when he stretched his arms. However, it was wide enough to fit six or seven people somewhat comfortably. There were boxes of old clothes, damaged hardware, and rotten food—though the nutrition bars seemed perfectly fine. Gennoveffa tore the wrapper off one and took a bite while they looked around.

Mafalda began sorting through the abandoned hardware. It was mostly burnt wires, engineer's tools, and some discarded chrome, presumably too damaged to remain in the wearer. David wondered if the safehouse had doubled as a blood clinic at some point. Perhaps that was how the Rivoluzionari paid their debts. Either way, what they left behind wasn't fit for much more than a trash bin.

David ran his hands along the walls. He wasn't sure what he was looking for, but if the occupants knew the safehouse wasn't a well-kept secret, perhaps they had a place to hide more valuable things, especially considering it lacked an escape route. Despite his optics, David's vision darkened as he walked along the walls. His fingers ran along steel, hard and cold, the implants in his hands gently scraping against the back of the wall. Then, something softer.

"Ah," he said, hesitating.

David switched from night vision to infrared. It took more power—something he had to be conscious of with synthetic eyes—but he needed to be sure. The safehouse lit up in a spectrum of blues bled into greens, with David's own hands appearing bright orange and red. He reached out and touched the wall, and the metal sheet easily folded away. Soil remained in its place. It was damp to the touch, dark blue to his eyes, and parts of it crumbled to the floor when he picked some up.

"Spit it out," Mafalda said, still focused on the hardware.

"I found soil."

"There's no soil *inside* the wall."

David tossed the handful he'd taken next to her. Mafalda was quiet for a moment while she investigated the lump.

David switched back to night vision, and the room snapped into a green, dim light.

Gennoveffa stepped toward Mafalda, head cocked. After a beat, she grunted. "That wasn't here when we controlled this spot."

Mafalda sighed. "The Rivoluzionari dug into the goddamn wall?"

"Looks that way," David said. "I bet they were trying to dig a passage out. Maybe to fix that problem you mentioned about having no escape plan."

"Rivoluzionari don't care about escape plans," Gennoveffa said. "You ever listen to their people? They always talk about toppling the old government, building the future by breaking what's old, and a bunch'a noise like that. The [morons] probably tried to collapse the civita to prove a point."

"Jesus," David said.

"You two better hurry up. If they've been digging in here, it could cave in at any time."

"David, help me carry out all of this stuff," Mafalda said. "I don't see anything else we need here."

"You got mixed up in some heavy shit, Maf," David said, tossing his coat over the back of a chair. They'd just returned home, carrying the old chrome they'd found. Since Mafalda had no space in the office, she laid out all the junk across the dinner table.

"I didn't mean to," Mafalda said. She sounded exhausted. "I thought I was looking for some sweet old lady's brother. Next thing I know, some Tigres have me cornered on Via Abbatantuono and inform me that I work for them now."

"I get it." David sighed. "You walk the path you're on—"

"When it's preferable to falling off," Mafalda finished. "The Tigres are paying us better, at least—double what Hachirō's sister offered—but they made it pretty clear that I couldn't refuse, either. The Tigres have calmed down a little since Mama Cinzia seized power, but they still know how to wet their hands. I wasn't about to test them."

David nodded. "I'm familiar with the type."

"Right. Anyway, I guess I don't feel too bad about it if Hachirō's helping the Revoluzionari. I'll refund his sister after this case is over. Don't need her sticking her nose into it before it's finished. Poor thing probably had no idea he was in such a mess."

"Good. Avoid the heroics."

"Exactly." Mafalda draped her arms over his shoulders and kissed him on the cheek. "What about your day? Did I miss anything while I was running around the city?"

He shrugged. "Mostly quiet. Some folks from Calanchi came about a missing child."

She raised her brows. "Calanchi. Sounds like a sweet end-of-year bonus."

"Mm-hmm. It'll be even sweeter if I can find the boy alive. Seems like he's got a knack for going into dangerous places. Likes to run off into the wilderness."

"None of that in Muro Etrusche. Runaway?"

"Most likely. Pinged Quinn about it. Tried p-trans, but they shut the door on my face to get out at five. Talked to some of the boy's neighbors but got little for it. His friend's acting weird, but not much I can do with that. Kids act weird by default."

Mafalda smiled at him. "Tomorrow's another day. What about the civita? Maybe the kid likes old stuff too."

"I thought the same thing. His padre shot down that idea. Might look around there anyway, ask some of the folks at the shops to keep an eye out for me... He loves the sea, so maybe he took a bus to Lago di Bolsena. It's not the same, but it's not too far. Maybe he's just at the beach there."

"Long trip to make on a hunch."

David sighed. "I know."

"You'll figure it out. If you don't, the kid'll probably die."

"Jesus, Maf."

Mafalda gave him another kiss, then took a seat in front of her bounty. "Are you awake enough to help me go through some of this junk? I need to find *something* before the Tigres come back tomorrow. I don't take either of them for the patient type."

"Sure." David took the seat beside her and picked up a bent piece of metal. "What's this, you think?"

"I think that's somebody's leg, David."

He set it back down and went into the wine cabinet. If he was going to deal with severed limbs, he would need some libations. When the latch clicked, Mafalda told him to get her a glass as well. He picked out a fruity Prosecco from Valdobbiadene and poured two glasses.

The next morning, David woke in a cool and empty bed, an alarm ringing in his cochlear implant. He unplugged a cable from the side of his head and checked his HUD—his optics were at full charge again. He dressed in a vintage gold sweater and blue jeans, brushed his teeth, and found his way back to the kitchen. Mafalda was seated in the same place she'd been the night before, sifting through the Rivoluzionari's old chrome, a tablet beside her transcribing her observations as she spoke.

"Coffee?" David asked, wincing at the morning light creeping through the window.

"Counter," Mafalda said. Her eyes never left her work.

"Ah, you already made some. Thanks. You sleep at all last night?"

"[A bit.]"

"Good. Find what you're looking for?"

"Think so." Mafalda picked up what looked like a piece of an old dermal grip—a flexible slab of metal shaped to fit in the palm of one's hand. David remembered seeing something similar on most of the soldiers he used to serve with. He tried to ignore the dried blood on its underside. "Take a close look here and tell me what you see. There's a logo in the center."

"It's pretty badly damaged," David said, taking the mod. His eyes adjusted and the image sharpened. "Can't make out the design, but I think the writing spells out *Zepponami*."

"That's what I thought. There's a clinic in Zepponami, and I think that's their signature. It looks like this to you, right?"

Mafalda grabbed the tablet and pulled the clinic's logo.

"Yeah, that's it. I didn't know there was a clinic in Zepponami."

"For a long time there wasn't. They opened shop in 2163, under new management as of this year. Not much news after that, but it seems they're still in business."

"Sounds promising."

She nodded. "Mm-hmm. If I can track down where these pieces came from, I might be able to figure out how the Rivoluzionari and Hachirō ended up in the same place. A bunch of them have that logo, as well as some of the mods you set aside for me last night. Most of the gear's damaged, but that looks intentional. Scratched off like they tried to do with this one. And, I'll remind you, our friend Hachirō is a clinic surgeon. Maybe he helped install some of these."

"Or helped remove them—"

"To replace old gear with the new stuff. The Rivoluzionari probably have a trove of fresh chrome ready to go that they're just dying to install or sell."

"And if Hachirō's got a clinic, he could do both. Install the pieces they need and sell the rest. Maybe even do a little scrapping on the side. The Revoluzionari aren't above looting their enemies for parts."

"He's the perfect partner for our favorite angsty rebels." Mafalda smiled, showing her teeth. "So, I'm headed to Zeppo shortly. The Tigres are already [on the way]. Are you able to come with us?"

David took a sip of his coffee and shook his head *no*. "Gotta' hit the streets."

"Right, the Calanchi kid."

"The boy's already been missing for a few days. If I don't make some progress today..."

"No leads?"

"Nothing overnight. No news from Quintino either, but I'm hopeful about the buses. I'll visit city center this morning to speak with somebody about their cameras."

"Right. Didn't you say the kid had an adventurous streak too? Maybe check around the civita while you wait to hear from trans-p. I know what you said—his father didn't think much of that—but the father's not the son. And, unless the kid's into clubs or gambling, the old village is the only interesting thing in this city. I ran a search while you slept just to make sure I wasn't forgetting something and came up dry. You know I'm right. Tourists don't come to visit *Muro Etrusche*."

"Some stop to look at the wall."

"Yes, but nobody comes all this way *just* to look at the wall. They all want to stand on top of it and look out over the city and Calanchi—not just the neighborhood, but everything beyond it. Come to think of it, maybe the kid went into Calanchi proper, exploring the Badlands. There's a river out that way, you said he likes the water, right? That's a lot closer than the lake."

"About the same distance."

Mafalda shrugged, and a flash of blue appeared over her eyes. "It's worth a shot. Anyway, the Tigres are here. Keep in touch, and ping me if you need anything."

"You do the same. Tigres are your friends now, but that can change in a heartbeat."

"I know. You forget, I grew up here, you damn [tourist]."

"Yeah, yeah. Just be safe out there."

"Okay, and you don't do anything fun while I'm gone." She kissed him, grabbed her jacket, and was out the door.

After breakfast, David caught a bus to the Muro Etrusche city center. It stood beside a large park, the building itself affixed to part of the wall. It was made of plasteel and self-healing concrete, styled to look like a classical Roman structure. Nothing else in the city looked quite like it.

David followed a hall all the way to the end, where it took on a much more sterile glow. The office of public transit was, in his experience, the best part of city hall. David didn't have any personal connections there, but it ran more like a company than a government institution. Requests and reports moved more quickly, and if all else failed, David could always grease somebody's palms.

It didn't take long for him to find somebody whose ear he could twist. He sent the rep behind the counter everything that he had on Ennio Segreti and suggested they keep an eye on buses heading out of the city and to run a search on the last week. They promised they'd monitor their security systems and let him know if the boy turned up anywhere. David hoped they'd have some footage of him boarding a bus a few days ago, but nothing came up in their searches. Still, having their surveillance network in his pocket was a hell of a lot better than nothing. Between them and the police's network, the boy was sure to show up on camera somewhere—if he was still in the city.

David returned to the park and found a cold bench to sit on. He leaned back under a barren tree and pinged Quintino. While he waited for a response, David glanced up at the wall behind the office buildings. He could just make out the tops of the old Etruscan buildings that remained in the civita above and the dozens of tourists already crowding along the top of the wall.

Quintino's message appeared on David's HUD.

[10:03] No word on your kid yet.

[10:04] Thanks for checking. Keep me in the loop.

[10:06] Good hunting.

David checked Ennio's social profile. There was little of note, but he set up a few scrapers anyway. If the boy posted anything, commented, or even just logged in, David would get a notification about it. With a bit of luck, maybe he'd catch a ping or see a picture of where Ennio was. It was all pretty rudimentary, but he'd solved cases with simpler tools. David regretted not setting any of those checks sooner, but after the business with the Tigres the night before, he never got the chance.

With that done, David walked up Via Sud, sharing Ennio's picture with anyone who would listen. That old-fashioned leg work took time, but David found that sometimes it led to places which normal means just couldn't. It was one of the reasons he and Mafalda found people who the police struggled with. Surveillance cameras and scrapers never quite delivered information with the same nuance that a real person could.

After a full day of talking to people around the city, David was left with little more than a hoarse throat. He had circled around the walls that cradled the civita and the hill it rested upon, winding back to the park in front of the city center. The sun was lowering once again, the day—and the year—nearing an end. David sat to watch the sunset from one of the park benches, his feet aching as he took his weight off of them. Throughout the day Mr. Segreti messaged him three times but David hadn't gotten back to him. He briefly considered doing so there in the park but decided against it. There were still a few hours left in the day. Still more time to give the man something other than bad news before the new year.

David checked the scrapers he'd placed on Ennio's accounts again. Still nothing. That was strange. The boy didn't seem particularly vocal on any of his feeds, but the days-long gap seemed out-of-character even for him. That could have meant a lot of things; at best he was enjoying a spontaneous vacation, at worst...

It was probably the simplest answer: he was just somewhere that didn't have a signal. If that was the case, Lago di Bolsena was back on the map. It was the closest place with spotty coverage that David could think of, especially once a person got away from the cities that bordered it. Other than that, there were some mines north of the lake, but half were shuttered and there was no way Ennio could sneak into the active ones.

Besides, why would he want to? The only adventure to be had in the mines was the thrill that at any point it might collapse on you. Even if the boy was a daredevil, David could think of plenty more entertaining ways to risk one's neck. Fireworks, for one. If ever a boy was going to mess around with some fireworks, it may as well be on New Years' Eve. The new year firework show was happening over the Badlands, so perhaps he went there to fire off a few of his own.

Although, the boy who fancied himself a Marco Polo didn't sound like the kind of person who messed around with fireworks.

David gave the case some more thought, then stood up from the park bench. He let his feet carry him deeper into Muro Etrusche, passing people he would have stopped to talk with earlier in the day. He traced the southern wall, bending around it where the south tower jutted from the façade like the turret of a castle wall. Traffic became heavier as he neared the eastern façade. David turned off his HUD so he could better focus on the cars, whose drivers seemed determined to ignore the traffic lights. He rounded another corner and approached the alley between the Madonna and the Poeta apartment buildings.

It was a long shot, but David was running out of time and had no strong leads. Ennio Segreti was adventurous, hadn't updated his feeds since he went missing, and hadn't appeared on camera for just as long. Quintino would have picked him up a dozen times over if the boy was walking around Muro Etrusche. The boy also hadn't been spotted on p-trans either, so he probably hadn't left the city. *However,* that Tigre Gennoveffa mentioned something that was replaying in David's head: kids snuck inside the wall on dares. It might be a waste of time, but David didn't have any other ideas left. Certainly none that got him back in time for Quintino's new year party. He pulled back the metal sheet that barely concealed the old hideout and stepped into the wall's breach once again, blinking away the darkness as his optics adjusted to the new environment.

The hideout was as they'd left it the night before, just a bit less cluttered since he and Mafalda had taken most of the scrapped hardware. David stepped over a box of nutrition bars toward the hole in the far wall, where he'd discovered soil protruding into the room. In the dim light, even with night vision on, it was difficult to see exactly what he was dealing with. He wished he'd thought of getting a flashlight somewhere, but he didn't have one at the house and wasn't sure where to get one. So many of those old tools had become mods instead, and while he saw the use in a wrist-light, he didn't have time to go to a clinic. His optics would have to be enough.

David ran his hands along the part of the wall he'd removed so easily the night before, feeling the cold, damp soil left behind. Then, he felt a gap. There was a hole in the wall, leading deeper into the façade and beneath Civita di Bagnoregio.

David paused. He knew what he needed to do, but he had no idea how safe it was. Everyone knew the civita was built on unstable ground and would have crumbled away long ago if not for the retaining walls. They had stopped the earth from spilling out, but it had continued to sink anyway. There was a good chance that if David went in there, he wasn't coming back out.

David checked his messages again. Nothing.

He called into the darkness, "Ennio?"

Again, louder and from his chest, "*Ennio!*"

Echoes reverberated around inside the wall. No response came.

"Son of a bitch," David muttered, then checked his messages again. Nothing.

David messaged Mafalda: *[19:08] If I'm not home when you get back, I'll need your help at Madonna's Bend.*

He didn't wait for her to respond. If she asked why, he'd tell her the truth, and she'd convince him not to go. That knowledge probably should have been enough to deter David from going deeper into the wall, but if his hunch was right, Ennio didn't have time for him to ponder any of that. David just needed to go, so that's what he did.

Darkness engulfed David as he crouched down low and crawled into the tunnel, the soil cold and damp around him. It clung to his hands and clothes as he stumbled in further.

David realized it wasn't a tunnel into the wall; he was inside the hill beneath the civita. He was in a mound of clay and soil and stone, with not a hint of the wall around him to be found.

"Fuck," David muttered, worry creeping into his chest.

He'd already come so far though. What was a little more? David pushed his way deeper into the wall—into the hill—feeling the narrow tunnel expand around him. It was just barely enough room for him to walk. David tried adjusting the settings in his optics to see better, but nothing seemed to help. He switched from night vision to infrared, and the tunnel lit up in a spectrum of blue and green. He could see in the pitch-black darkness, finally. The muddy walls revealed themselves, as well as some kind of support beam placed every dozen feet. He switched back to night vision, returning to darkness. He didn't dare leave his optics running on infrared for too long.

"Ennio!" David called again, pushing through a narrow section of the tunnel. The hill pressed against him on all sides. If it got much tighter, he'd have to turn back around.

"Ennio!" he called again. David flashed infrared, making sure he wasn't in a maze. The tunnel stretched onward, twisting, slightly rising. There was only one way so far, but it was impossible to tell exactly where he was or what direction he was going. The map on his HUD wasn't working properly when he tried to orient himself with it, so he turned it back off.

"Ennio!" he called again. A message from Mafalda appeared in the corner of David's vision, only partially loaded before he completely lost his signal. Whatever she'd told him, it wasn't getting through the wall and earth around him, though he could imagine her objections well enough.

"Ennio!" he called again. The tunnel felt as though it were constricting around him again, forcing him to crouch lower. Much more, and he would need to crawl forward again. David's foot caught on the uneven ground, and he fell against the wall. It sagged under his weight. His hands stuck to the mud as he pushed himself away and stepped forward with soil clinging to his palms and under his fingernails.

David stopped there, hunched over in the darkness, and turned on his infrared. He blinked, and the world was illuminated in blues and greens. The light was almost blinding compared to the total darkness he'd been walking in. If Ennio wasn't close, David decided, he would turn around. The narrow tunnel and the way it gave under his weight was beginning to make him wonder if he'd come too far already. He didn't even know if Ennio was really there.

The tunnel, however, was changing. It was now just wide enough for two people to uncomfortably walk side-by-side. The ceiling arched upward, just enough room for him to stand upright. He walked forward, and the tunnel opened further. The narrow passage gave way to a small cavern—almost a proper room. He switched on infrared again. Plasteel support beams were positioned along the walls and center of the hollow, surrounded by mud and rock. A few appeared to be slipping, fixed at awkward angles as the earth shifted around them. In the center of the room was a small desk. It lacked any chairs, but it had been in use recently. There was an old electric camping lantern set atop it, turned off and illuminated in green through David's optics, but still warmer than anything around it.

Underneath the lantern was a folder with papers sticking out of the top. Around the desk, there were three sleeping bags. Two were rolled up tight, placed on top of a rug. The third was blue and cold, but open like an unmade bed. Somebody had been in it recently.

When David was sure nobody else was in the area, he decided to peek at the documents. He switched off his infrared and flicked the lantern on. It cast a bright electric glow over the muddy room. David picked up the folder and revealed the documents within. They were handwritten in Italian, and David's optics helped translate the text, appearing like captions across the page, but they made little sense. The text spoke of cicadas, Mars, and—for some reason—the Bible. David had attended his family's church back in the States, and he didn't remember any stories of Jesus or his apostles dealing with such things. Perhaps they looked up at the sky and saw Mars, or heard the cicadas as they came out of the ground to breed, but was any of that worth writing in the holy book? It made no sense...

...Unless it wasn't *supposed* to make sense. After all, the Rivoluzionari made the tunnels, and they weren't exactly known for their legal dealings. If anyone found the documents, presumably, heads would roll. So, how should they protect themselves? Just like their colored rags in the safehouse, it was a code.

One of the papers was missing. The final page in the folder ended on an incomplete sentence, and for all the confusing text in it, that was something even its author hadn't done anywhere else. There was more of the cryptic file out there somewhere.

David snapped a photo of the documents with his optics and then folded them into his pocket. As he did, he noticed something about the sleeping bags that he hadn't been able to see when he was looking at everything in infrared. The two rolled up were simple, no frills, made-for-warmth camping equipment. The open one on the ground displayed the colorful silhouettes of t-rexes, pterodactyls, and other dinosaurs.

"[Who are you]?" a voice asked in Italian.

David spun to face the voice, muscles coiled. He nearly fell over when he saw a young boy in muddy, wrinkled winter clothes. His blond hair was a mess, shaved and pushed to the side to make room for a large implant that coiled around his ear and the side of his head. The boy carried a lantern like the one David had found and had a backpack slung over his shoulder.

"Ennio Segreti?" David asked.

"[Yes. Who are you?]"

"Holy shit," David said, laughing. "My name's David. I run a small agency. My wife and I find things, people—"

"You're a *private eye*?" he asked, switching easily into English.

"Yeah." David showed the boy his card. "Your parents asked me to come find you. Didn't you hear me calling your name earlier?"

The boy tapped the implant on the side of his head. "I had the volume turned down. You're kind of quiet still. One sec—and that should be good. Sorry, I'm still getting used to this."

"No, you're fine."

"Hearing is nice, it's just a lot sometimes. [Too much.] The sounds are so much clearer than they were with my old gear." The boy's lips curled into a frown. "How long have I been here?"

"A few days, I think."

"Hm. I lost track of time. Without the sun..."

"Didn't you get hungry?"

"I brought sandwiches." The boy patted his pack, then added, "I *had* sandwiches."

David took a step forward. "How about you get your things, and we'll get out of here."

"Do I have to? I still haven't explored all the tunnels. The main one branches off in a few places and—just look here," Ennio said, and walked toward the desk. The mud stuck to his shoes as he did, making wet, sucking sounds each time he raised a foot. Ennio opened his bag and took out a piece of paper. It was the Rivoluzionari's missing page, the end of whatever manifesto they'd left behind. Ennio had drawn a map on the back of it. "I came here with my friend Vanni, but he was too scared to come into the tunnels, so I decided I would make a map for him to show him it was safe. But—"

"Wait, Vanni knew you were here this whole time?"

"Yeah. You know him?"

David sighed. "Kind of. Boy, keep him around. Your friend's loyal to a fault."

"Vanni didn't tell you where I was?"

"Nope. I suspected he knew something, but he never said a word. Vanni must have thought he'd get you in trouble or something."

"Oh, wow. You must be a really good private eye then. I don't think anyone else knows about this place. Aside from the people who came before us, but they're gone now. Built all this and just left, kind of like the Etruscans and the civita, right? Unless... Did you make these tunnels, [mister]?"

"No." David laughed. "Somebody else did, and we don't *know* that they're gone for good, so we should start moving. The hill is unstable, and your parents are worried sick, Ennio."

"I guess," Ennio said, drawing out the words in a barely conceded defeat. He put the map back into his backpack. "I didn't mean to scare them. I was just having so much fun exploring the tunnels. It was like discovering a new world, hidden right next to the city! Imagine what else is out there, under the earth, under the seas..."

"You're right about that. Come on, and hold on to that map. I've got a friend in the police who would be really interested to see it, I think."

"The [police]?"

"Yeah. For now, come on, let's get moving. You know the way out?"

Ennio scoffed. "I was the first to map the tunnels of Muro Etrusche! Of course I know the way out. It's this way, but will you fit? The tunnel gets really, *really* small in a few places. I had to *squeeze* through."

"I got here, didn't I? You go first, grab your sleeping bag and lead the way, Mr. Explorer."

As he followed Ennio toward the exit, David checked his messages. Still no signal. Mafalda's last message was still grinding, attempting to load. He hoped everything went okay in Zepponami—but he couldn't do anything about it either way until he got Ennio home. He wished he could tell her what had just happened. The sheer luck of running into the boy. If he'd given up at any point earlier in the tunnels... Ennio would never have appeared on any of the surveillance systems he'd gotten Quintino or p-trans to look for him with. Perhaps the boy would have come out on his own eventually, but David was glad he wouldn't have to take the chance on that.

The tunnel widened, then it constricted on them again. David was ready to have to crawl on his stomach when Ennio stopped, a hesitant groan escaping his lungs like a whisper.

"What's wrong?" David asked.

"This is the way out. I know it."

"Okay."

"But the tunnel ends here."

"What?" David pushed past Ennio and reached ahead. Sure enough, a fresh mound of mud and rock was blocking their path. A chill ran down David's spine. "Shit. I was *just* here."

"[Mister] Private Eye David, are we stuck?"

David tried clearing away some of the debris with his hands, but more mud replaced what he could excavate, and there wasn't much room to put the earth he pulled aside. He stopped, fearing that he was only weakening the tunnels' already tenuous structure.

"You mapped all the tunnels out, right?" David asked.

"Most of them. I'm still missing—"

"Is there a way to get to the surface? Or at least a path up to where I might be able to get a signal out to somebody?"

"I can get us higher up, but I wasn't able to get a signal from there."

"Maybe I can," David said. He tapped the side of his head. "Some of this chrome is courtesy of the U.S. military. My signal's got pretty good range."

"*Cool*. Isn't every American in the military, though?"

"What? No. Most aren't."

"Oh. Vanni said that all Americans were required to serve in the military, though."

"Nah. Come on, let's hurry."

Ennio led the way deeper into the tunnels, their shoes squelching in the muck. David tried his best to stay in good spirits, but they were stuck inside the hill, and he still didn't have a signal to get help. He'd messaged Mafalda about coming after she got back, but what would she do with that? He regretted not being more detailed. However, if he'd waited any longer, he might have run into that cave-in trying to get to Ennio and never would have found him. Although, he wasn't sure that dying in the hill with the little explorer was much better.

What other choice did he have? David had set on that path the moment the idea crept into his head and he wandered back toward Madonna's Bend. He took a deep breath, raised his lantern, and followed Ennio into the black.

The tunnel was mostly straight, angling slightly upwards, sometimes bending or splitting off into new directions. Ennio was focused on his map, checking it often, whether or not there was a change in direction. David began to believe that the boy just wanted an excuse to reference it.

"Hey, [Mister] Private Eye David—"

"Just David is fine," he interrupted.

"Okay. [Mister] David, what other mods do you have from the military?"

"Not much anymore. They deactivated most of 'em."

"Vanni says the U.S. military turns its soldiers into robots with all the mods they make them install."

"Vanni's got a fun imagination. Most soldiers only have the basics: a dermal wrap and a pair of lenses, if they consider the soldier's personal wear inadequate. You can opt into some other things sometimes, but that's about it for most of 'em."

"Hm. Vanni said he saw a woman from the U.S. and her whole body was synthetic, almost. All she had left was her head. No, he said all she had left was her *face*. The rest was all metal and wire."

"Maybe she was a specialist. Depending on what your job is, you might need more chrome. Most soldiers don't need much, but some—like divers—require a lot of support to do their job well. Every country pumps their funding into creating the best divers they can. They always end up looking like some new model of sports car, lean and sleek and shiny."

"Were you a diver?"

"Do I look 'lean,' 'sleek,' or 'shiny' to you, boy? Nah. Don't tell anyone, but I was low-level counterintelligence. Used to have all kinds of gear for collecting and protecting data in the Net. I could disrupt weaker systems with a thought. They also put a dagger in my wrist just in case somebody sent an assassin after me," David held the lantern up to a long seam on his right arm where they'd implanted the mod. It was still in there, just disabled. "I wasn't a diver, but I worked with them often. Kept them safe while they fought the real battles."

"*Woah*. Did you ever have to fight an assassin?"

"No," David lied. "How're we looking? Getting close to the surface?"

Ennio slowed down while he looked at his map. He pointed to a crudely drawn line around the center of the paper. "We're here, on *Via Covo*."

"You named the tunnels?"

"Yeah! This is the longest one. Most of the others are really short. Via Covo is kind of like the [highway]. Everything connects to it."

"Okay, good. So, we're close."

"Well, maybe. I haven't been to the end of Via Covo yet."

"Well, let's hurry up. I don't like all this mud in my boots."

The tunnel narrowed again as they pressed onward. However, as David crawled through a slender corridor on his stomach, he noticed the earth around them seemed drier than before. Rather than squelching beneath their weight, the soil crumbled. It didn't instill a great deal of confidence, but it was certainly *something*.

At some point, Ennio started drawing on his map, announcing they'd crossed into a place beyond what he'd seen. David let him keep leading the way, pausing briefly for him to add to the drawing as they traveled through the tunnel. It seemed to make the boy happy. Besides, there was no chance he'd be able to pass Ennio in the narrow tunnel anymore. David felt lucky he could fit at all.

David checked his signal as he crawled through the earth. It had transitioned from no signal to a weak one. He urged Ennio on, but they could only move so quickly, crawling as they were. Then, a barrage of messages spilled across his HUD, all from Mafalda, each increasingly more anxious than the last. A few missed calls were mixed in too, but he couldn't tell yet if she'd left any voice messages. He replied. David and Ennio were crawling through the tunnels for another fifteen minutes before the text was finally delivered.

Detective Quintino Kimedi returned to his office and hung up his coat. As always, the new year was bringing out the worst in people. In the past week alone, he'd responded to numerous calls involving thieves, vandals, abusive partners, and one arsonist who tried to escape on a trans-p bus. They might have delivered him to police custody if he hadn't threatened the driver. Quintino almost felt pity for the young man. Sure, he'd burnt down half of the café on Via Leggièri, but nobody deserved a corporate cell. The office of public transit liked to make an example out of people who went after them—in any form. There was nothing Quintino could do about it, though. Business as usual.

He sat back in his chair, listening to the sounds of the station. People spoke on their old-fashioned desk phones, tapped away at their keyboards, and a screen down the hall droned on about the rising cost of living. One panelist raised her voice and cursed out the prime minister just before they cut to commercial break.

"Detective Kimedi," a man's voice came through his cochlear implant, "Somebody's asking to talk with you, says it's urgent."

Quintino glanced at his monitor. Still no hits on that kid David had asked him to watch for. "Tell David I don't have anything for him," he said.

"It's a woman, sir. Mafalda De Campo."

"Maf? Fine, send her over to my comms."

There was a pause as the tech transferred Mafalda's call, then an audible click as it connected.

Mafalda didn't give him a chance to say hello. "I think David's inside the wall." The words shook her voice and tumbled forward like vomit.

"In that breach along the eastern façade, you mean? Did we forget to tape it?"

"No, I think he's found a way *inside* the wall, not just in that hole. Look, he sent me these messages just now." A notification appeared on Quintino's lens, asking if he would accept a file from Mafalda. He did, and a stream of messages between Mafalda and David appeared. "The timestamps are all off. I got the last message he sent some fifteen, twenty minutes after he sent it. He's talking about how he can't get out at Madonna's Bend. He's trying to find a way through the civita."

Quintino sat forward. "What do you mean by 'through the civita?' The Porta San Maria's the only way in and out of there."

"Obviously. Look, I don't know what's going on either, but I think he's in trouble. He said to meet at Civita di Bagnoregio, so that's where I'm going. I'm asking you to come with me."

"Okay. Should I bring anything? Anyone?"

"I don't know, Quinn."

Quintino stood and grabbed his coat. "I'll figure something out. And I'll grab a booster. That should help us reach him if he's got a poor signal. Maybe some pylons too. The place will be crawling with tourists. I'll meet you at the Piazza San Donato in thirty or so—depends on traffic."

"Thank you, Quintino," Mafalda said, then disconnected.

The tunnel that David and Ennio walked through ended in a small room. It was much like the one where the Rivoluzionari had set up some kind of camp, but there was barely enough space for both him and Ennio to stand. One of the walls had a ladder propped against it, and another bore a collection of drills, chisels, and a small battery-powered air purifier.

"I guess this is the end of the tunnels," David said, breathing heavily. He was sweating from the effort of crawling through the mud, and the air was thin. He turned on the purifier, and a steady hum filled the space as it began to work.

"[Mister] David," Ennio said, sweating along his brow, "what now?"

"Give me a minute," David said, catching his breath.

David's HUD told him that his signal was medium strength. Not ideal for a call, but his messages shouldn't be delayed anymore. It also meant they were probably close to the surface. He opened his map, copied his location, and sent it in a message to Mafalda: *[22:43] I've got a better signal now. Near the civita. Get Quinn and come here.*

[22:43] You're at the fucking museum?

[22:43] I'm underneath it.

[22:44] What do you mean underneath it? I don't see you.

A call came over David's HUD. He accepted it, but Mafalda's voice came in too choppy to hear most of what she said. Despite that, she sounded furious—and loud. He knew what she was asking, for the most part.

"I'm underground," he said slowly, hoping that would help her understand through their poor connection. "I'm under the civita. I'm as far as we can go… I'm underground."

The call disconnected.

"Any luck?" Ennio asked.

"Working on it," David said.

"You don't have any MG tech that can help us out? Can you blow a hole in the roof?"

David turned on his infrared. The colors were slightly warmer than in the lower tunnels. The ladder and tools shone back at him in a dark blue. "I can't 'blow anything up,' but I can tell you that nobody's used these tools recently."

Ennio picked up one of the drills. "I guess that's good. We don't want to see the people who made these tunnels, do we?"

"We don't," David agreed.

Another call came in over David's comms. He accepted it.

"David, are you hearing me?" Quintino's voice came in loud and clear. He must have been using some kind of signal booster to strengthen their connection. Weird that he would carry one of those around, but David wasn't about to complain.

"Sì, I hear you," David said.

"Good. [Now, what the hell have you gotten yourself into?]"

"Long story short, I found the boy, but we're stuck in tunnels beneath the civita. We're close to the top, but there's no way out. I need you to dig."

"[There are no tunnels under Civita di Bagnoregio.]"

David sent him his live feed. Everything his optics recorded appeared in a window on their call. The video quality was terrible, but hopefully it would be the proof Quintino needed to shut up and get them out. A few moments passed, and David heard the detective talking with a few other people, the shuffling of bags, and a long dramatic sigh. David cut the feed as Quintino began to talk again, and the call quality became dramatically better.

"—practically under Antica Civitas. The town won't be happy if I start digging there."

"This is the highest we can go, and if I'm being honest, the air isn't so good in here, Quinn. We're fine for now, but if you could hurry, that'd be great."

David shot the boy a smile to ease the impact of what he'd just said, for what little good that was. To his credit, Ennio took the information in stride. He'd probably already guessed they were in trouble, anyway.

"Give me a few minutes. I'll see what I can do."

Quintino hung up the call.

"I have some friends coming to get us," David told Ennio. "It shouldn't be much longer."

"They won't damage the civita getting us out, will they?"

"I'm sure they'll do their best to avoid it."

David and Ennio were struggling to stay awake. He couldn't tell if they were so tired because it was so late or if the air purifier wasn't working properly. Lethargy was one of the first signs of carbon monoxide poisoning. Or was it simply a lack of oxygen? With the entrance collapsed, no fresh air was getting in. Even before, there wasn't much airflow, especially this far into the tunnels. How much more time did they have?

David tried talking to Ennio about his map, which kept the boy going for a few minutes, but eventually they both ran out of things to say about it. They moved on to football, and Ennio had a laugh about how Americans played football with their hands. It wasn't funny—it never had been—but David laughed along to make sure the boy kept talking.

After a while, Ennio got quiet, then asked, "Is your [police] friend going to take my map? The tunnels aren't supposed to be here, so they're going to... You know..." Ennio trailed off, as if he couldn't remember what he was trying to say.

"You have any lenses in those eyes?"

Ennio shook his head. "I'm getting mine when I turn sixteen, Papà said."

"Give the map here," David said, holding out a hand. Ennio took the map from his backpack and handed it over. "My optics have a camera. I'll just take a picture for them, and maybe one of what's written on the back, just in case."

"The writing is [nonsense]."

"I know, but just in case. I'll make sure to send the map to you later, when we're above ground. That way, *if* they confiscate it for a while, you'll be able to redraw it later." He handed Ennio his map back. "Maybe keep the map in your bag for now though. I won't say anything about it if you don't."

"Deal," Ennio said, a sly smile spreading across his face.

[23:38] Quinn's got help. We're going to start drilling.
[23:39] Thanks, Maf.

"Ennio," David said, "Scootch back."

"[What?]" Ennio grumbled.

"Come on, boy. Unless you want to be underneath the drill."

As if on cue, an engine stirred above ground, and a grinding sound filled the chamber. Ennio rolled over onto his side, eyes closed, and thumbed a dial on his cochlear implant.

David grabbed Ennio by his ankles and dragged him into the tunnel. He shouted, and the drilling became louder. Just as David got Ennio into the tunnel, a piece of soil and stone fell to the floor, landing with a heavy, wet *smack*. They watched quietly as more pieces of the makeshift ceiling crumbled and fell. The drilling sound became louder, and larger pieces of earth fell. Then, there was a strand of light, and some of the debris contained frigid brown grasses.

"David!" Mafalda's voice came over the drilling, just barely.

[23:46] It's good to hear your voice, he replied over text.

It took a few minutes to carve out a hole big enough for them to climb out of. David extended the Rivoluzionari's ladder and sent Ennio up first, then followed behind. They emerged behind the old museum, a small stone building with tendrils of ivy creeping along its façade. Crisp winter air wrapped around them, and a crowd surrounded their exit, barely contained behind a circle of police pylons. Bright yellow light created a barrier between them that read *Police Line: Do Not Cross*. The horde respected the line, but they demanded answers. Some wanted to know who he and Ennio were, others were furious about the damage to the civita, but most just wanted to know about the tunnels. David couldn't blame them.

David found Maf within the pylons. He rushed to embrace her and felt her tears on his cheeks. As they parted, she slapped his shoulder and said, "If you ever do that again, I'll kill you."

"Love you too," he said, laughing.

"Your clothes," she said, unable to properly finish the sentence. David glanced down at himself and resigned that his sweater and jeans were probably ruined.

"[You're lucky you ended up *outside* of Antica Civitas,]" Quintino said, walking over to them. "[I can ask for forgiveness about the alley. But if you were just a few meters further, I don't know. The historians are nasty in a fight.]"

"Grazie, Quinn," David said, reaching out to embrace his old friend. "Sorry about your New Year's party."

"What's to be sorry about?" Quintino asked, and opened his coat just enough to show David the flask tucked into his pocket. "[You think any of this is going to slow me down?]"

"Hm. I should have known better."

"[You absolutely should have, you damned fool.]"

"What about Zepponami?" David turned back to face Mafalda, remembering she'd gone after Hachirō with the Tigres. "Did you find your surgeon?"

"Hot on the trail," she said. "Ran into some complications, but they're taken care of now."

"Anything I should worry about?"

She shrugged. "The enforcers took care of it."

"Okay, well, I need to get Ennio home," David said. "I told his family I'd get in touch with them by the new year. They're worried sick."

"I'll drive," Mafalda said, raising her hand to reveal the keypad on her fingertip. "You look exhausted, and I'm not letting you slink off on your own again so soon. I haven't given you nearly enough shit for what you did yet."

Quintino took a swig from his flask and handed it to David.

"Grazie," David said, then took a drink.

As he handed back the flask, an eruption shot off nearby—somewhere beyond the eastern façade. A few seconds later, fireworks danced in the black sky, blooming in all manner of reds, yellows, and greens. They illuminated the Badlands, leaving trails of grey smoke barely visible in the night sky. Drones joined the show and created giant projections of men and women dancing among the fireworks, transforming into wolves and leaping through the light show. Finally, the figures took on the form of ancient Roman gods and goddesses. The image of Mars rode a chariot through a red explosion, and Pomona pulled a lemon from a yellow one.

"[I've never seen this from so high,]" Ennio whispered. Even the crowd around them had been lulled into a hush. "[Can we stay and watch it, Mister] David? Just for a minute."

"Sure, boy," David said, and put an arm around Mafalda, pulling her close.

"You're getting mud all over me," she said, laughing, and rested her head against his shoulder.

Content Warnings List

Digital Extremities is intended for mature audiences and contains some content and references that may be off-putting to some readers. I've included a list of content warnings below with as few spoilers as possible:

"Alone / Together" contains on-page depictions of depression and off-page references to miscarriage.

"Buying Time" contains off-page references to a character's death.

"Atlantic Essentials" contains alcohol abuse.

"36 Broadway Avenue" contains violence and depictions of mental health complications.

"The Beast of Longyearbyen" depicts death.

"Fireworks Above the Badlands" contains on-page descriptions of being trapped underground and off-page references to terrorism.

About the Author

Adam Bassett is an author, designer, and illustrator from Northern New York. His writing has also appeared in anthologies such as *Nature Erupts* (Two Doctors Media) and previously volunteered as the editor-in-chief at Worldbuilding Magazine, where he published fiction and non-fiction in select issues.

Follow him @adamcbassett on Twitter, Threads, or Instagram; or visit adamcbassett.com.

Acknowledgements

This collection of stories would not have been possible without the help of my editors Beth Heyn, B.K. Bass, and Natasha Vella. I'd also like to thank to Stephanie Vislay and Julia Rylen of Alex Parker Publishing, who helped review "Alone / Together" and included it as part of the *Rare* short story anthology.

Additional thanks to my beta readers Alex Atkins, Eliza Leone, Emory Glass, Matthew Gorman, Taylor Frymier, Tricia Jackson, and W. Yu Phen. You all helped me improve these stories and gave me the courage to see it through.

To my advance readers who read the book early, thank you for your taking a chance on it. Your enthusiasm and encouragement has been incredible.

I'd also like to thank my cover artist Igzell, and character artist Red Pharaoh (whose work you can find on Campfire in this book's Extras). Together, their work helped bring these stories to life—and sometimes even affected the way certain descriptions were written during final edits!

www.ingramcontent.com/pod-product-compliance
Lightning Source LLC
Chambersburg PA
CBHW022124310726
48972CB00007B/2183